the
sonoran
grill

by
mad coyote joe

photography by
christopher marchetti

Northland Publishing

The book is dedicated to the people I love most: my mother, Pat Daigneault; my father, Joe Daigneault; my children, Katie Rose and Joey; and most of all, to my wife and best friend, Kathy.

The publisher wishes to thank Tycha's Beyond the Border in Cave Creek, Arizona, and Kitchen Classics in Phoenix, Arizona, for generously contributing their beautiful dishes to the pages of this book.

The text type was set in Minion and Formata
The display type was set in Founders Caslon 12
Composed in the United States of America

Printed in China

All cooking temperatures in this book refer to the Fahrenheit scale.
The use of trade names does not imply an endorsement by the product manufacturer.

ISBN 10: 0-87358-759-6
ISBN 13: 978-0-87358-759-4

07 08 09 10   10 9 8 7

Library of Congress Cataloging-in-Publication Data

Mad Coyote Joe.
    The Sonoran grill / by Mad Coyote Joe ; photography by Christopher Marchetti.
        p. cm.
        ISBN 0 87358-759-6 (alk. paper)
    1. Barbecue cookery. 2. Cookery, American—Southwestern style. 3. Sonoran grill (Television program)   I. Title.
    TX840.B3 M22 2000
    641.5'784—dc21
                                99-056082

contents

introduction
while the grill is getting hot

About a million years ago, man discovered fire, and the grill was born soon after, along with cooking in general. I believe that on that day, the message "Grilling is good" was imprinted on our DNA, never to be erased. This means two things:

First, it's in our nature to cook over an open fire.

Second, through grilling you fill some sort of primordial need that dates back to when your family tree didn't have any branches.

Even though we now stand upright, there is a little caveman in all of us that still wants, and needs, to cook outside, you know—grilling, smoking, and barbecuing!

My first cooking memory is from when I was five years old, in Salt Lake City. My parents had gone away and a nice, older lady was watching us kids. I told her I was hungry and she said, "Well go make yourself something to eat." I remembered seeing my father do this, so I took a piece of white bread and cut a thick slice of Cheddar (I believe it was Tillamook Sharp Cheddar). I placed the cheese on top of the bread, turned on the broiler, and watched through the oven window. I can still see the cheese melting and bubbling as it started to brown. I took it out of the oven. The bread was warm, and where the top wasn't covered with cheese it was toasted dark brown. The cheese was

melted to perfection on top and just below that wonderful, crunchy crust was a hot and gooey center. It was the best cheese sandwich I ever ate.

A year later we moved to Scottsdale when my dad started a steel company. I soon discovered not only my lifelong love, but the only thing hotter than the Arizona sun: chile peppers. It all happened when my dad brought home one of his foremen, Andy. Andy was from Mexico, and his wife brought a treat for dinner: green chile burros. Fresh, hand-made tortillas wrapped around fire-roasted green chiles made up into a thick, savory stew. This was not only our first taste of Mexican food, it was also our first taste of chiles of any kind. And boy, howdy, were they ever hot. So hot, in fact, that my brothers and sisters wouldn't eat them. But me: I loved them. After that I was hooked for life.

In eighth-grade metal shop (age 12), when Mr. Webster asked what we wanted to make, most of the other boys decided to make signs with their families' house numbers. I asked if I could make a barbecue. Mr. Webster's solution was to take one of those old square salad-oil cans from behind the cafeteria and let me cut a hole in the side. Across the hole we stretched thick wire. I took it home and told my dad that we were going to do some serious grilling.

I filled my oil can barbecue with charcoal, doused it with lighter fluid, and lit that baby up! After about ten minutes, the oil can started melting and my dad put it out with the garden hose. I was heartbroken.

But a few days later, my dad went out and bought a brand new, two-burner gas grill (Thanks, Dad!) and my grilling career was off and running. I was soon grilling hamburgers and hot dogs for the whole family.

Then, one day, my older brother, Mike, showed us a trick he had learned at his job as a busboy at The Pink Pony restaurant in old-town Scottsdale. He put garlic salt on the hamburgers. Wow! We had never had anything like that before and were all very impressed. For a while he got to cook the family hamburgers. So as not to be outdone, I came up with my first recipe. I took a piece of Cheddar cheese (I believe it was Tillamook Sharp Cheddar; it was my dad's favorite), and a green chile out of the can. I cut the chile in half, stuffed the cheese inside it, and molded a hamburger (five kids—we ate a lot of hamburgers) around the chile, and then grilled the hamburger to perfection. Just imagine: charred on the outside, but when you bit into it, green chile and melting cheese, too! I can still remember my mother telling me that I should enter my recipe in the Pillsbury bake-off.

In high school and college I worked in several of the restaurants around Scottsdale.

In my late twenties I started the Mad Coyote Spice Company and the name Mad Coyote Joe just sort of stuck. Well, one thing led to another, and soon I was judging chile cook-offs, winning national awards for my spice products, and even writing for national food magazines. Then, one day

in June of 1997, I came home and checked my answering machine.

"Mad Coyote Joe, this is Don McClure down at KNXV TV. We're going to start a new cooking show on grilling and I'm thinking that you just might be the guy to host it."

They could have hired a professional chef with a culinary degree, but they were looking for a regular guy with a passion for Southwestern foods— and a good knowledge of grilling, smoking, and barbecuing—that would cook the way real people cook.

Our goal on *The Sonoran Grill* is not only to take the mystery out of Southwestern grilling, but also to approach cooking in general from the standpoint of an everyday guy. There is not a dish in this book that the average person cannot cook, if they just take their time and follow the recipe. Cooking is a chance to spend time with the people you care about. It's easy, entertaining, and most of all, fun. Remember, you can do this. One of the most satisfying things that happens to me is when I'm out somewhere and a viewer comes up to me and says, "Hey, Joe; I don't know very much about cooking, but I made your Mayan Sea Scallops, and they turned out perfect." They know exactly how I felt, at the age of five, standing on a chair in my pajama bottoms, looking into an oven at my very first culinary masterpiece.

And finally, no discussion of Sonoran cuisine would be complete without an understanding of daily life in Sonora, Mexico. I'd like to share a morning I spent in 1993, sixty miles south of the Mexican border, below Nogales, in the small farming village of Terrenate. The following is from my journal:

It's 7:00 A.M. The sun is just behind the mountains east of town. The sky is clear and turquoise blue, with a few lazy clouds overhead. The air is warm and perfumed with the scent of the orchid trees and spring flowers that are in bloom everywhere.

The house we are in was built out of adobe brick in the late 1890s and has been modified by each generation since. We are sitting at a small wooden table in a modest but clean kitchen that looks out onto a large garden. The sparrows and cardinals out back are chirping and singing, echoing the excitement of this beautiful spring morning.

Our host, Norma, is in her late sixties and has a smile that never seems to leave her face. She speaks no English.

Santiago has been gone since first light, just as he has each morning for the past forty years. By now he's walked the four miles to his fields; fed, watered, and milked his cows; and is on his way home, with the milk in a large steel milk can. He will go back later and work his crops and orchard, but now, it's time for breakfast.

"Quiéres café? (Do you want coffee?)," Norma asks.

Coffee in northern Mexico is served two ways. The most common is from instant coffee, very dark with lots of sugar. But this morning we are in for a real treat! In a typical gesture of Mexican hospitality, Norma got up at first light to roast coffee from fresh green coffee beans, shaking them back and forth in a large black iron skillet over the coals from the mesquite fire that warms the kitchen; they slowly start to brown. The beans turn the color of milk chocolate after about twenty-five minutes.

Now she adds about a cup of the raw sugar granules, so common to this part of Mexico, and continues to roast the beans for a few more minutes. The beans turn dark brown, almost black, and are removed from the heat immediately. About a half cup at a time, they are run through a coffee grinder that looks like an old-fashioned meat grinder. Norma then puts a handful of the fresh ground coffee into the kind of coffee pot we use for camping here in the U.S., and puts it on the fire. The coffee is served hot, dark, and sweet in a large mug and you are quite sure it is the best cup of coffee you have ever had. As is the custom, Norma will serve her adult guests and her husband first and then she will eat with the children. The breakfast: homemade refried beans; large, handmade tortillas (very thin); scrambled eggs; avocado; fire-roasted green chiles. Along with this, chile tepins, lime, salt, and salsa cruda are served and eaten at a typically relaxed Mexican pace.

That's the Mexico I think of whenever I'm talking about or cooking Mexican food. Combine that feeling with my love of mouth-watering smoked meats and the fact that just about anything can be cooked in your own backyard on the grill, smoker, or barbecue and you're ready for a little Sonoran Grillin'!

So light the grill, invite some friends over, pour a few ice-cold margaritas, sit back, relax, smell the chiles roasting over the mesquite charcoal, and wow your friends with a dinner that you thought was beyond your reach. Very soon the best restaurant in town will be your own backyard!

chile peppers

The chile pepper is the soul of Sonoran cooking. Hot, mild, sweet, pungent, dried, pickled, ground, smoked, roasted, fresh, canned, or frozen, it has been the dominant flavor of the Sonoran diet for the last five hundred years.

From the Indians to the missionaries to cattlemen, right on down the line to the backward flow of Californians, someone new is always moving to this beautiful desert. Each group has found, or brought, their own special use, and love, of chiles, constantly adding new ingredients, and redefining Sonoran cooking. Although the cuisine changes over time, the one constant is the use of chiles. This re-inventing is precisely what gives Sonoran cooking its unique personality.

Whether it's something as basic as green chile or one of the new fusion dishes like Mesquite-Seared Aji Tuna Steaks with Habanero-Lime Butter, these wonderful dishes all find their basis in chiles.

fresh chiles

anaheim

The most common green chile available in the Sonoran Desert. About the color of the skin of a fresh lime, 5 to 6 inches long, and usually mild, but watch out: these are sometimes very hot. Often used for roasting or Chiles Rellenos.

habanero

The hottest chile in the world. The name means "from Havana." Colors include any combination of yellow, orange, red, and green. In this part of the world, they grow to roughly the size of a ping-pong ball, but in the Yucatan they are known to grow as large as a medium-size bell pepper. Once you get past the heat, this delicious little wonder has a rich, sweet, vegetable flavor that is unmistakable. Great in salsas or roasted. I use it to help add a Caribbean flavor to dishes and sauces.

jalapeño

The most popular of all chiles: dark green, bullet-shaped, about 2 to 3 inches long. A good medium heat. Great in salsa, chile, or any place you want heat. The darker the hotter, and the black ones: watch out!

poblano

This is my favorite chile for roasting or stuffing: heart-shaped and deep forest green, 4 to 6 inches long, hotter than the anaheim. I like to roast these with just about anything.

serrano

Great in salsas and on sandwiches, or eaten raw, this chile has a distinct flavor. Hotter than the jalapeño, it is about 2 to 3 inches long, 1/2-inch across, bullet shaped.

dried chiles

I've said it before and I'll say it again: If you want to know about Mexican foods, learn about dried chiles!

ancho
The dried form of the poblano: deep, dark, reddish brown, and heart-shaped. About 4 inches long and 3 inches across at the widest part. Anchos add a rich, earthy flavor to sauces and moles. It is the most widely used dried chile in Mexico.

chipotle
The chipotle is a dried, smoked jalapeño. About 3 inches long and light chocolate brown. Its hot smoky flavor is unmistakable and a must for sauces, salsas, and Sonoran barbecue rubs.

chile de arbol
Chile de arbol is a thin, bright red chile about 3 inches long and about 1/3 of an inch wide. Very hot, used to brighten up hot sauces and salsas. Also a great addition to marinades.

guajillo
Guajillo chiles are shaped like an anaheim: blood-red, 5 or 6 inches long, about 1 1/2 inches wide, with a medium heat and mildly sweet full-bodied flavor. They are used in sauces, salsas, and stews. This chile is wonderful when used with roasted meats, especially pork.

new mexico mild
Also known as chile colorado, this is the chile that you see in ristras hanging on the porches of the old adobes in New Mexico: deep red, about 6 inches long, and 1 1/2 inches wide. Full of red chile flavor, it is the best chile for all-purpose chile powder and the secret to my award-winning Texas-Style Red Chile.

pasilla, or chile negro
The pasilla ("little raisin") is a dark, reddish brown, wrinkled chile; hence the name. It is about 6 inches long and about 1 inch wide. A little richer and deeper flavored than the ancho, it's great in sauces and mole; also very nice with seafood.

chile tepin
These little fireballs are harvested in the wild in Sonora, Mexico. They are bright red, round, and about 1/3 of an inch across. Related to the chile pequin, they are red hot and most commonly served on the side with tacos, soups, and stews.

tools

There is a reason that professionals use all the right tools: they make the job a lot easier. Here are a few tools that I simply cannot do without.

comal
The comal is a round, flat, iron griddle used in Mexico for heating and making tortillas.

lime press
The lime press is a little like a garlic press: It presses all the juice out of limes.

forged knives
After you've used forged knives you will wonder how you ever got along without them. They not only make cutting easier, they make it faster and more precise.

potato ricer
A potato-ricer is a press that will make the best mashed potatoes you've ever eaten. It's fun and very fast.

pump oil–sprayer
There are so many places that you need a little oil. I don't like the canned stuff at the store. How old is it? What's the quality? I prefer to choose which oil I want for which job.

steak spatula
A good-quality steak spatula is an absolute must for grilling fish and a handy all-around grilling tool.

pizza stone/baking stone
This stone changes your grill into an outdoor cooking center. It is necessary for grill-roasting, indirect cooking, and grill-baking. My advice: Buy one!

A bowl of steaming homemade soup

after a hard day feels like a great

big hug from grandma and a wink from your sweetie all

soups

rolled into one hearty bowl of delicious satisfaction. Here

in the Sonoran Desert, we serve it with a squeeze of

lemon or lime and a crushed chile tepin.

joe's chicken soup

Around my neighborhood, this chicken soup is said to be able to raise the dead. When the temperature drops and the days are gray, you'll be sure to find a big pot of it simmering at my house. The secret to making good chicken soup is making good chicken broth. Start with an older chicken, preferably a "Grade A" whole roaster. Fresh, not frozen. Freezing dries out the natural juices. The outside of the chicken should be white, not yellow, and it should smell fresh and clean.

STOCK

2 whole large fresh chickens
4 to 6 fresh lemons
2 white onions, with skins, cut in half
3 fresh carrots, washed and sliced
3 ribs celery, with leaves, coarsely chopped
5 to 6 sprigs fresh parsley
¼ teaspoon crushed red pepper
6 whole cloves
2 bay leaves
2 teaspoons dried thyme
8 whole black peppercorns
2 teaspoons kosher salt
2 (14-ounce) cans chicken broth
1 gallon pure water

SOUP

5 stalks celery, finely diced
1 (14-ounce) can diced tomato
(I like S&W brand)
2 bunches fresh spinach, washed
1 bunch fresh cilantro, minced

GARNISH

Lemon wedges
1 white onion, finely chopped
8 to 10 chile tepins

Wash the chicken with fresh lemon juice as soon as it comes home. Cut up 2 fresh lemons per bird and rub all over and inside; do not rinse off lemon.

Use a fresh lemon half to rub down your cutting board. Cut the chickens into pieces. Remove any fatty-looking skin and discard. The next step may be omitted but I highly recommend it. With a heavy cleaver, break the bones in the legs, thighs, wings, backs, and breast.

In a very large stock pot, place chicken and all vegetables and spices for broth. Open cans of chicken broth, remove fat, and add to stock pot; add water to cover chicken. Over medium heat, bring to a slow boil. Reduce heat and simmer for 1½ hours. In the first hour of cooking, place the pot half on and half off the burner and do not stir. This will cause the impurities to rise to the side away from the heat. A froth will appear: Remove with a large spoon and discard. Remove from heat.

Remove all large chicken pieces from broth and pour remaining liquid through a strainer into a bowl. Place in refrigerator to cool. Remove all meat from bone and discard skin; be careful to check for small pieces of bone. Cut meat into ½-inch cubes. After broth has cooled, spoon off all fat that has risen to top. Pour broth into a large stock pot and add chicken, celery, and tomato. Over medium-low heat, simmer for 45 minutes or until celery is tender. Salt to taste. In a large soup bowl, place approximately 10 to 15 spinach leaves and 1 teaspoon chopped cilantro. Ladle in soup and serve immediately. Serve with lemon wedges, chopped white onion, and 1 chile tepin per bowl; be careful, these little devils are red hot!

Serves 8 to 10.

gazpacho

In The Mad Coyote Café (Kathy's Deli), we always ran out of our refreshing Gazpacho. It was a local favorite.

4 cups tomato juice
2 cups diced tomatoes
1 cucumber, peeled and diced
1 clove minced garlic
1 avocado, peeled and cut into ½-inch cubes
½ green bell pepper, cut onto ¼-inch pieces
½ large white onion, finely chopped
½ jalapeño pepper, seeds removed and finely chopped
Juice of ½ lemon
Juice of 1 lime
2 tablespoons light olive oil
¼ cup fresh parsley, chopped
2 tablespoons red wine vinegar
1 teaspoon fresh basil, chopped
2 teaspoons Tabasco sauce
½ tablespoon dried Mexican oregano
1 teaspoon honey
Salt to taste

Put everything in a large bowl. Put bowl in the refrigerator. Go take a nap with someone you love. When you wake up the soup is ready and so are you.

Serves 4.

posole

Posole, the classic American Indian soup, is eaten throughout the Southwest and all through Mexico. It is the perfect slow-cooker meal and works well with leftover pork or poultry. This is where our leftover Thanksgiving turkey usually goes. I have received more compliments on this dish than on any other I cook!

SOUP
2 pounds roasted pork or any
cooked poultry
3 (14½-ounce) cans white
hominy, drained
1 teaspoon whole Mexican oregano
3 cloves fresh garlic, minced
1 teaspoon ground cumin
⅓ cup New Mexico mild
red chile powder
2 (48-ounce) cans chicken broth

GARNISH
1 purple cabbage, finely chopped
1 white onion, finely chopped
1 bunch red radishes, washed
and thinly sliced
1 bunch fresh cilantro, washed and diced
1 tablespoon chile tepins
(cayenne pepper may be substituted)
2 fresh limes, cut into wedges
(Key limes if available)

In a large slow-cooker place pork or poultry, hominy, oregano, garlic, cumin, chile powder, and chicken broth. Heat on medium for 5 to 6 hours or longer. Stir occasionally. Serve in large soup bowls with a little of each of the following: purple cabbage, white onion, red radish, and cilantro.

Crush 1 chile tepin or add a pinch of cayenne pepper and a squeeze of fresh lime.

Serves 8 to 10.

opposite: *Smoked Brisket Caldillo (recipe page 99) and Posole (recipe above).*

menudo

If you've never tried menudo, I recommend it. The flavor is wonderful and, in this part of the world, it's the only cure for a hangover! It can be found in good Mexican restaurants every Sunday morning.

3 pounds tripe, well washed
3 white onions, chopped
3 cloves garlic, minced
1 teaspoon whole Mexican oregano
1 tablespoon salt
1 (28-ounce) can white hominy
1 bunch cilantro, cleaned
and finely chopped
2 fresh limes, cut into wedges

In a large stock pot, bring the tripe, 2 onions, garlic, oregano, salt, and water to cover to a boil. Simmer on low all day (at least 6 hours). Add a little water now and then as needed.

When the tripe is tender, remove it from the pot. Cut into ½-inch cubes and return it to the pot. Add hominy and cook for 1 hour more.

Serve in large soup bowls with a little cilantro, a little onion, and a lime wedge on the side.

Serves 6.

grill-roasted kabocha soup

This soup is also great made with pumpkin.

SOUP
1 medium kabocha or other winter squash
4 tablespoons sweet butter
4 scallions, finely chopped
1 medium white onion, diced
3 shallots, minced
3 cloves fresh garlic, minced
½ teaspoon paprika
½ teaspoon cayenne pepper
½ teaspoon cumin
½ teaspoon Mexican oregano
4 cups chicken broth
1 teaspoon dark brown sugar
½ bunch fresh cilantro, finely chopped
¼ cup heavy cream
Salt and pepper to taste

GARNISH
3 tablespoons freshly squeezed
lime juice
1 cup sour cream

Preheat grill on highest setting. Cut the kabocha in half and remove seeds. Place in grill cut side up. Set burner directly below kabocha on lowest setting. Bake for 45 minutes or until kabocha is soft. Remove from grill and let cool.

In a medium stock pot, sauté scallions, onion, shallots, garlic, and dried spices in butter until onions are soft and translucent. Scoop out three cups of grilled kabocha and add to stock pot. Add chicken broth, brown sugar, and cilantro. Stir in the squash and let simmer for about 15 minutes. Purée hot soup in blender, a little at a time until smooth, pouring blended soup into a serving bowl. Whisk in heavy cream and season.

Serve in large soup bowls with a dollop of lime cream.

Serves 4.

sonoran pottage bonne femme

Pottage Bonne Femme is a classic French soup. The name basically means "Good Woman Soup." As always, I've given it a Sonoran twist. Don't let the name fool you: This soup is quick, easy, and most of all, delicious.

SOUP
3 cloves garlic, peeled and chopped
1 large shallot, peeled and chopped
1 large leek, chopped
1 white onion, chopped
3 tablespoons sweet butter
2 tablespoons flour
6 cups chicken broth
4 cups peeled, cubed, and
rinsed white potatoes
1 cup poblano chile, roasted and peeled
½ cup heavy cream
1 tablespoon finely chopped fresh thyme
½ teaspoon finely chopped lavender
Salt and freshly ground black pepper
to taste

GARNISH
1 cup sour cream
1 chipotle chile, (canned, not dried)
with a little adobo sauce*
Fresh thyme, finely chopped

Sauté garlic, shallot, leek, and onion in butter until translucent. Add flour and fry until roux is a light beige. Add chicken broth and potatoes; simmer until potatoes are extremely soft. Purée with an electric hand whisk or blender. Stir in chile, cream, thyme, and lavender. Add salt and pepper and adjust seasonings.

Whisk sour cream and chipotle with adobo sauce together. Ladle soup into bowls; top with a dollop of chipotle cream and a sprinkle of fresh thyme.

Serves 4 to 6.

Adobo sauce is the sauce that chipotle chiles are canned in.

wonton soup

These wonton have a much fresher taste than store-bought or those found in most Chinese restaurants.

24 wonton (recipe below)
2 (14½-ounce) cans chicken broth
Approximately 1 cup chopped
mixed vegetables, such as bok choy,
spinach, green onion, snow peas,
or whatever you like

Bring a large pan of salted water to a boil. Drop wonton into the boiling water. When they rise to the top of the water, reduce heat to low and simmer for 4 minutes.

In a separate pot bring chicken broth to a boil, drop in vegetables, and simmer for 2 minutes. Spoon into large soup bowls and spoon in 4 to 6 wonton per bowl with a slotted spoon. Enjoy.

Serves 4.

wonton

Wonton are easy: The secret is to use raw pork and cook it in the wrapper.

1 pound ground pork
½ pound cooked medium shrimp, peeled,
tail removed, and chopped
¼ cup minced water chestnuts
¼ cup minced green onion
2 tablespoons soy sauce
1 tablespoon freshly grated ginger
1 package wonton wraps
1 egg white, beaten

Mix together pork, shrimp, water chestnuts, onion, soy sauce, and ginger.

Place 2 teaspoons of the mixture in each wonton wrapper, brush edges of wrappers with egg white, and press together. If you like, brush the pointed edges with egg white and fold in. Deep-fry or use in soup.

Makes 30 to 35 wonton.

Here in the Sonoran Desert, the sun

shines about 350 days a year. We raise

some of the finest produce in the world: sweet corn, fresh

salads

herbs, fragrant garlic, and a host of greens. Our tomatoes

are big, ripe, and bursting with flavor and our cilantro,

tomatillos, and chiles are unbeatable. These easy salads will

transform everyday dinner into a gourmet feast.

asian beef salad with thai chile dressing

If you're a little crazy about grilling (and I know you are!), you'll love this spicy Asian salad. It has a great grilled-beef flavor and yet is very light and refreshing. Just the right thing on a hot summer day.

THAI CHILE DRESSING
1 Thai chile, chopped
(remove seeds if you don't like HOT!)
1 large clove garlic, minced
2 tablespoons soy sauce
2 tablespoons fresh lime juice
1 tablespoon sugar
2 teaspoons sesame oil

SALAD
1 pound London broil, grilled medium
rare, sliced into thin strips
½ cup red onion, julienned
¼ red bell pepper, julienned
¼ cup fresh cilantro, chopped
4 cups napa cabbage, sliced thin
2 tablespoons dry-roasted peanuts,
coarsely chopped
4 lime wedges for garnish

In a blender, blend dressing ingredients together. Toss beef, red onion, bell pepper, and cilantro; add dressing and toss again. Divide napa cabbage on four chilled salad plates. Top with beef salad, sprinkle with peanuts, and serve each salad with a lime wedge on the side.

Serves 4.

chinese asparagus salad

Try this fantastic Asian twist on everyday asparagus!

SALAD
1½ pounds fresh asparagus
(the thinner the better)
2 teaspoons white sesame seeds
(untoasted)

DRESSING
5 teaspoons dark sesame oil
1 tablespoon sugar
2 teaspoons soy sauce
2 teaspoons white vinegar
1 teaspoon brown sugar

Discard woody ends of asparagus and cut asparagus into 1- to 1½-inch-long pieces. Bring a pot of water to a boil and fill a bowl with ice water. Drop the asparagus into the boiling water for 1½ minutes. Remove with strainer or tongs and drop into the ice water to stop the cooking. Leave in the ice water for 1 to 2 minutes and then pat dry with a paper towel.

Whisk dressing ingredients together; let stand for 10 minutes for flavors to blend. Whisk again, add ¾ of the sesame seeds, pour over the asparagus, and toss. Cover with plastic wrap and set in the refrigerator for 3 hours. Remove from the refrigerator, remove plastic wrap, toss well, add remaining sesame seeds, and serve.

Serves 6 to 8.

baby spinach salad

This salad is a great side dish for a grilled fillet of beef or a nice piece of fish. Served with Soy-Ginger Vinaigrette (recipe page 31), it's Don McClure, our technical director's, favorite salad.

1 pound baby spinach
¼ red onion, julienned
1 ounce enoki mushrooms
2 teaspoons black Japanese sesame seeds

Submerge spinach in a bowl of water and rinse well. Place in salad spinner; spin until dry. Toss spinach, onion, and mushrooms. Top with black Japanese sesame seeds.

Serves 6 to 8.

nopales salad

Nopales—prickly-pear cactus pads—are delicious. . . . but . . . if not cooked correctly they are a slimy mess. So follow my recipe and you'll find a wonderful new treat from the Sonoran Desert. This recipe works well with store-bought, bottled nopales, but reduce amount used in recipe to three cups, due to shrinkage of nopales in cooking.

6 cups nopales, cut into ½-inch squares
3 bunches green onion
7 tablespoons salt
1 fresh jalapeño pepper, diced
(do not remove seeds)
2 medium plum tomatoes, diced
¼ cup finely chopped white onion
½ bunch cilantro, chopped
Juice of 2 Key limes
½ teaspoon Mexican oregano

In a medium stock pot, cover the nopales with at least 3 inches of water. Add 1 bunch of green onions and 2 tablespoons of the salt and bring to a rolling boil. Let boil for ten minutes. Remove from heat and pour into a colander. Discard onions; rinse nopales in cold water until cool. Repeat the boiling twice using remaining 2 bunches of green onion and 4 table-spoons salt. This will remove the viscous material (slimy stuff) from the cactus pads. The nopales will now be about half the amount you started with.

Mix nopales, jalapeño, tomatoes, white onion, cilantro, lime juice, oregano, and remaining teaspoon salt. Let stand for 45 minutes for flavors to blend. Serve at room temperature.

Serves 8 to 10.

opposite: *Grill-Roasted Habanero Pork Tenderloin (recipe page 76) with Sonoran Tamarind Sauce (recipe page 56), Nopales Salad (recipe above), and Ensalada de Orzo Diablo (recipe page 24).*

ensalada de orzo diablo

If you're tired of everyday pasta salad, give this one a try. But watch out: It's got a real bite!

SALAD

3 cups orzo
1 each, yellow and red bell pepper
cut into ¼-inch pieces
2 habanero chiles, diced
(keep the seeds for unreasonable heat)
1 cup whole medium, pitted olives
1 cup golden raisins
½ cup chopped Italian parsley
⅓ cup diced red onion
10 ounces frozen sweet peas,
cooked and chilled
Salt and pepper to taste

VINAIGRETTE

⅓ cup red wine vinegar
½ cup chopped cilantro
1½ teaspoons Dijon mustard
1½ teaspoons dark brown sugar
2 cloves garlic, minced
1½ teaspoons salt
1 teaspoon freshly ground black pepper
⅔ cup olive oil

Cook the orzo in salted boiling water for 8 to 10 minutes until just tender.

Remove from water, rinse well in warm water, and drain.

In a large salad bowl, whisk all vinaigrette ingredients except oil together and then drizzle in the oil while whisking. Add the orzo and toss well.

Add all remaining ingredients and toss again. This salad is best if chilled overnight in the refrigerator to allow the flavors to marry. Serve at room temperature.

Serves 8 to 10.

black bean and white corn salad with ancho-cilantro vinaigrette

I like to serve this colorful salad with any Southwestern grilled meal. It's an unexpected treat at a "potluck." Crunchy, spicy, and light, it can be made up a day in advance.

SALAD

3 (14-ounce) cans black beans, drained and rinsed
1 pound frozen white corn, thawed
½ cup minced red onion
½ cup finely chopped green onion
2 cups chopped ripe tomatoes

VINAIGRETTE

1 dried ancho chile, rehydrated in water for 45 minutes, seeds removed, and finely chopped
⅓ cup seasoned rice vinegar
1 teaspoon sugar
⅓ cup freshly squeezed lime juice
½ teaspoon salt
½ teaspoon medium ground black pepper
⅓ cup light olive oil
1 bunch fresh cilantro

Combine beans, corn, and both onions in a mixing bowl.

In a separate bowl, combine ancho chile, vinegar, sugar, lime juice, salt, pepper, and olive oil. Clean the cilantro and remove any leaves that do not look fresh. Set aside 15 to 20 sprigs of cilantro for garnish. Finely chop remaining cilantro and add ½ cup to dressing mixture. Whisk dressing and add to salad, toss well, then add tomatoes and gently fold in. Garnish with cilantro sprigs. If storing overnight, refrigerate but serve at room temperature.

Serves 8 to 10.

warm chèvre and sundried tomato salad

Try springing this salad on your friends that don't like goat's cheese. It adds a mild, creamy flavor to this fresh-tasting salad. With a fruit plate and a cold white wine, this salad is the perfect Sunday brunch on a nice, spring day.

1 (6-ounce) roll of chèvre (goat's cheese)
1 egg
2 tablespoons water
1 cup seasoned bread crumbs
¼ teaspoon cayenne pepper
Nonstick vegetable spray
4 cups spring mix assorted salad greens
1 avocado, sliced
1 roasted red bell pepper, sliced
4 sundried tomatoes, finely chopped
Grill-Roasted Golden Pepper Dressing
(recipe page 31)

Place pizza stone on grill, light burners, and turn to low. Turn off the burners directly below the pizza stone, allow grill to slowly heat up to about 400°, and adjust heat to maintain 400°. If you only have one burner you may need to elevate a wire rack to about 1 inch above the pizza stone to indirectly bake this.

Cut the cheese into 8 rounds. Whisk together the egg and water. Mix the bread crumbs and cayenne together. Dip the cheese in the egg wash and then in the bread crumbs. Spray a nonstick cookie sheet with the vegetable spray.

Place the cheese rounds on the cookie sheet and bake on the pizza stone for 10 minutes, or until soft and lightly browned. Remove from cookie sheet and set aside.

Divide the spring mix on 4 large chilled salad plates. Top with warm rounds of chèvre, avocado slices, roasted red bell pepper slices, and a sprinkle of sundried tomatoes. Drizzle with Grill-Roasted Golden Pepper Dressing.

Serves 4.

assorted berry-fruit salad in spiced sauvignon blanc

Try this colorful fruit salad after an elegant dinner. The presentation is stunning.

4 peaches
½ pint strawberries, cleaned and sliced
1 cup sugar
1 (750-ml) bottle of sauvignon blanc
3 cinnamon sticks
Zest of ½ orange
½ pint blueberries
½ pint raspberries
1 cup green grapes
Zest of one lime
Slices of lime for garnish
Sprigs of mint for garnish

Gently drop the peaches in a pot of boiling water and blanch for 20 seconds. Remove from water, drain, and peel with a paring knife. Slice the peaches, discarding the pits. Place in a mixing bowl, add the strawberries, and cover with ½ cup of the sugar. Let stand for 15 minutes.

In a medium saucepan, over medium heat, simmer 1 1/2 cups of the wine, remaining ½ cup sugar, cinnamon, and orange zest for about 10 minutes. Allow to cool.

Place the peaches and strawberries, blueberries, raspberries, grapes, and the lime zest in a large glass bowl with the spiced wine and the remaining wine from the bottle. Cover with plastic wrap and chill for about 2 hours. Serve in champagne flutes. Garnish each glass with a slice of lime and a sprig of mint.

Serves 6 to 8.

warm wild mushroom, toasted macadamia nut, and roquefort salad

For that special evening when everything has to be just right, try this delightful salad. The combination of the mushrooms and the macadamia nuts will make your guests think that you are some kind of a cooking genius.

1 pound assorted wild mushrooms,
stems removed (shiitake, oyster,
chanterelle, morels)
3 tablespoons safflower oil
3 tablespoons walnut oil
2 tablespoons Spanish sherry vinegar
1 teaspoon Dijon mustard
6 cups spring mix assorted salad greens
¾ cup toasted macadamia nuts
6 ounces Roquefort cheese, crumbled
Salt and pepper to taste

Sauté the mushrooms in the oils over medium heat. Let cool for a few minutes and stir in vinegar and mustard. Arrange the spring mix on salad plates. Using a slotted spoon, top the greens with the mushrooms, macadamia nuts, Roquefort, and salt and pepper. Serve immediately.

Serves 6 to 8.

sweet red chile-toasted pecans

Forget croutons; try these sweet little devils on your next salad. They also make a great snack.

1 cup pecan halves
1 teaspoon safflower oil
2 teaspoons sugar
1 teaspoon raw sugar
1 teaspoon brown sugar
½ teaspoon kosher salt
1 teaspoon New Mexico mild
red chile powder

Toast pecans over medium heat, just until fragrance releases. Add oil and stir to coat. Sprinkle with the sugars and salt and stir until sugars start to caramelize and melt. Sprinkle with red chile, stir, and remove from heat to a plate. Allow to cool before serving.

tabouli salad

Sometimes you don't feel like meat. This salad is so refreshing and delicious, we eat it about once a week during the summer along with hummus, a few kalamata olives, and warm pita bread. To add a grill-roasted flavor to our Mediterranean meal we make baba ghanouj: a classic Middle Eastern dish made with eggplants, tahini, garlic, parsley, and lemon juice. Yum...

SALAD
1 cup Bulgur wheat, dry
1 ½ teaspoons kosher salt
1 ½ cups boiling water

DRESSING
¼ cup extra-virgin olive oil
¼ cup freshly squeezed lemon juice
1 tablespoon freshly squeezed lime juice
2 cloves garlic, finely minced
½ teaspoon dried mint

FINISH
1 cup plum tomatoes, diced
1 cup English cucumber, diced
½ cup scallions, finely chopped
1 bunch Italian parsley, finely chopped
2 teaspoons kosher salt
Freshly ground black pepper to taste

Pour the bulgur into a mixing bowl, add the salt, and pour in the boiling water. Cover with plastic and let soak for 30 minutes.

Whisk dressing ingredients together and stir into the bulgur. Allow flavors to blend in the refrigerator for 3 hours.

Carefully stir in finishing ingredients. Taste to correct seasoning.

Serves 8 to 10.

toasted sesame coleslaw

Wow your friends with this Asian twist on everyday coleslaw.

SALAD
½ green cabbage, cored and
sliced very thin
½ red onion, sliced very thin
1 large carrot, grated
3 tablespoons black sesame seeds
3 tablespoons dry-roasted peanuts

DRESSING
⅓ cup rice vinegar
1 ½ tablespoons dark sesame oil
1 tablespoon sugar
2 teaspoons Dijon mustard
1 teaspoon salt

Toss cabbage, onion, and carrot well. Whisk dressing ingredients together. Add dressing to cabbage mixture, and toss well. Refrigerate for two hours to allow flavors to blend.

Just prior to serving, add the sesame seeds and peanuts, toss well, and enjoy.

Serves 6 to 8.

vinaigrette

Once you've mastered your own homemade dressings you'll say good-bye to bottled salad dressing forever. This basic vinaigrette is a good place to start.

⅓ cup balsamic vinegar
½ teaspoon Dijon mustard
¼ teaspoon sugar
½ teaspoon dried chervil
½ teaspoon chopped fresh parsley
1 clove garlic, minced
Pinch of cayenne pepper
Salt and freshly ground pepper to taste
¾ cup extra-virgin olive oil

Whisk the vinegar and mustard together until well mixed, and whisk in sugar and seasonings. Slowly pour in the oil while whisking, and let stand at room temperature for at least 30 minutes. Whisk just prior to serving.

Makes about 1¼ cups.

soy-ginger vinaigrette

Any time you're serving a meal with an Asian twist, try this vinaigrette on a spinach salad. We love it with Mesquite-Seared Ahi Tuna Steaks (recipe page 85): Yumm . . .

2 tablespoons Japanese soy sauce
1½ tablespoons dark sesame oil
1½ tablespoons seasoned rice vinegar
2 dashes Arizona Gunslinger Sauce
(or your favorite hot sauce)
1 teaspoon sugar
1 Thai chile, finely chopped
2 teaspoons freshly grated ginger

Whisk all ingredients together.

Makes about ½ cup, but a little goes a long way.

grill-roasted golden pepper dressing

An elegant yet simple salad dressing with a great grill-roasted flavor.

1 yellow bell pepper
¼ cup chopped, fresh basil
3 cloves garlic, minced
2 tablespoons seasoned rice wine vinegar
1 tablespoon fresh squeezed lemon juice
1 teaspoon dark brown sugar
½ teaspoon Arizona Gunslinger Sauce®
(or your favorite hot sauce)
¼ cup avocado oil
Pinot Gregio, for thinning the dressing

Roast the bell pepper until charred on all sides, place in a plastic bag and twist down, removing all the air. Let stand for 5 minutes. Remove from plastic bag, and discard stem, seeds, and peeling.

Place the roasted bell pepper, basil, garlic, vinegar, lemon juice, brown sugar, and hot sauce, in the blender and blend well. While blender is running, slowly add avocado oil. If dressing is too thick, thin with a little Pinot Gregio.

Salsas are the heart of Sonoran

cooking. Fresh homemade salsa is

nothing like its inferior competitor: store-bought salsa.

You won't believe what Seafood Salsa will do for any

grilled fish, and Smoky Ranchero Salsa is an absolute

must for a Sonoran breakfast. We always have two or

three fresh salsas in our refrigerator.

two-chile salsa with avocado

On Sunday mornings I like to invite my producer over for breakfast. I usually call and say, "Bruce, come over and I'll cook you a ham steak bigger than your head." His standard reply: "Only if you're making your Two-Chile Salsa!"

1 habanero chile, diced
1 serrano chile, diced
2 tomatoes, diced
1 avocado, peeled, seeded, and cut
into ½-inch cubes
½ white onion, minced
2 cloves garlic, minced
½ bunch cilantro, finely chopped
Juice of ½ lime
2 teaspoons kosher salt

Gently fold all ingredients together and let flavors blend for 2 hours in the refrigerator.

Makes about 1¼ cups.

avocado-tomatillo salsa

If you're ready for the next level of salsas, give this one a try: It's fantastic. Also, try serving it with roasted pork, chicken, or fish.

5 tomatillos, husked and cleaned
½ white onion, chopped
¼ cup chopped cilantro
1 clove garlic, diced
1 serrano chile, stem removed
1 teaspoon salt
2 tablespoons water, plus extra as needed
1 ripe Haas avocado, peeled and cubed

Place tomatillos, onion, cilantro, garlic, chile, salt, and 2 tablespoons water in a blender. Purée until smooth. Add avocado and purée until smooth. Add more water if needed. Salsa should be a thick liquid, about the consistency of catsup.

Makes 1½ cups.

avocado-corn salsa

This salsa is an excellent side for any grilled fish or meat. Also try serving it with tortilla chips and margaritas as an appetizer.

2 cups white corn, drained
3 Haas avocados, peeled, seeded, and chopped into large chunks (about ¾ inch)
¼ cup canned or fresh roasted green chiles
1 jalapeño, diced
¼ cup chopped white onion
½ ripe plum tomato, seeded and diced
1 tablespoon fresh chopped cilantro
½ teaspoon crushed red chile
1 clove garlic, minced
Pinch oregano
Pinch black pepper
Pinch celery salt
Salt to taste
Squeeze of lime

Gently fold all ingredients except salt and lime together in a mixing bowl. Salt to taste and top with lime juice. Let stand at room temperature for ½ hour before serving.

Makes 4 cups.

cranberry-serrano salsa

We serve this unexpectedly tart salsa in place of cranberry sauce at Thanksgiving.

2 cups chopped cranberries
1 serrano chile, diced
¼ cup finely chopped white onion
¼ cup finely chopped fresh cilantro
Juice of 1 lime
2 tablespoons dark brown sugar
2 teaspoons freshly grated ginger

Mix all ingredients together. Refrigerate for ½ hour before serving to allow flavors to blend.

Makes 3 cups.

salsa for grilled lobster

I made this rich salsa to go with grilled lobster, but it goes well with any grilled or roasted seafood!

3 large ripe plum tomatoes, diced
½ English cucumber, peeled and finely diced
salt (at least 2 teaspoons)
Freshly ground black pepper to taste
2 jalapeño peppers, stems removed, finely diced
1 large white onion, finely diced
1 bunch cilantro, cleaned and chopped
4 large Haas avocados, cut into ¾-inch chunks

Place the tomatoes and cucumber in a large bowl and top with the salt and pepper. Let stand for 10 to 15 minutes. Place all other ingredients except avocado in a bowl. Mix well and fold in avocado. Cool in refrigerator for about 1 hour before serving.

Makes about 4 cups.

seafood salsa

The little fish taco stands along the Sea of Cortés in Mexico use this salsa to give their tacos that special taste. The secret is the cucumber. This salsa goes well with any fish.

4 to 6 large ripe tomatoes, diced
1 large cucumber, peeled, seeds removed, and chopped
2 jalapeño peppers, stems removed, and chopped
1 large white onion, chopped
1 bunch cilantro, cleaned and chopped
Salt, more than you think (at least 2 teaspoons)

Place all ingredients in a large bowl and cool in refrigerator for about ½ hour before serving.

Makes 4 cups.

opposite: *Grilled lobsters with Salsa for Grilled Lobster (recipe above), Seafood Salsa (recipe above), Yucca Root with Tangerine-Grapefruit Sauce (recipe page 52), and Grilled Pineapple with Pink Grapefruit, Lime, and Dried-Cherry Glaze (recipe 131).*

salsa cruda

This fiery salsa should be in every Sonoran cook's recipe file. It's quick, easy, and delicious.

3 whole serrano chiles, diced
½ white onion, diced
2 large, ripe plum tomatoes, diced
¼ loosely packed cup diced fresh cilantro
1 teaspoon light olive oil
½ teaspoon salt
1 tablespoon water

Mix all ingredients together and let stand 1 hour to blend. Serve with fresh tortilla chips and margaritas.

Makes 1¼ cups.

smoky ranchero salsa

This smoky, fiery salsa is a must with a Mexican breakfast.

Nonstick cooking spray
6 tomatillos, husked and rinsed
5 to 6 cloves garlic (do not remove peel)
1 medium white onion, diced
3 chipotle chiles (canned, not dried)
1 tablespoon adobo sauce
1 cup hot water
½ loosely packed cup chopped
fresh cilantro
½ teaspoon salt

Lightly coat a large, heavy skillet with nonstick cooking spray. Brown the tomatillos and sauté until soft. Remove tomatillos from skillet and then brown the garlic and onions. Peel garlic and place it and the chiles, adobo, water, tomatillos, onions, cilantro, and salt in a blender. Blend on high until smooth. Serve warm. Keeps for 2 or 3 days in the refrigerator.

Makes 2 cups.

mango-habanero chutney

This treat from India takes on a Southwestern flavor with the addition of a habanero chile.

2 large mangos, peeled, pitted,
and cut into chunks
½ cup water
1 cup dark brown sugar
½ cup apple-cider vinegar
1⅓ cups golden raisins
Juice of 1 lime
1 tablespoon honey
1 teaspoon cinnamon
1 teaspoon ground cloves
1 teaspoon ground cardamom
1 teaspoon ground ginger
1 habanero chile, seeded and minced

Mix all ingredients except habanero together. Bring to a boil over medium heat; reduce to low and simmer for 15 minutes. Let cool and then stir in habanero.

Makes 2½ to 3 cups.

salsa de la casa

Tacos just aren't the same without this very spicy, all-purpose hot sauce.

1 (8-ounce) can tomato sauce
2 teaspoons crushed red chile
1 teaspoon whole Mexican oregano
¼ teaspoon salt

Mix and let stand. This sauce keeps in the refrigerator for about a week.

Makes 1 cup.

You're on your way to the Fourth-

of-July potluck supper. Do you want

to bring the same old baked beans or macaroni-and-

side dishes

cheese? Think of the look on their faces when you come

strutting in with Yucca Root with Tangerine-Grapefruit

Sauce or Confetti Rice Pilaf. This chapter also contains

what I believe to be the best condiment on earth,

Habanero-Lime Butter! And you'll finally learn the secret

to making a perfect Chile Relleno.

borracho beans

You'll find these fantastic beans also served under the name "charro beans." All your friends will be asking for this recipe.

1 pound dried pinto beans
1 tablespoon white vinegar
1 bottle of Dos Equis Beer
½ pound bacon, fried, crumbled and drained
(Reserve 2 tablespoons of drippings for finish)
2 white onions, diced
1 tablespoon safflower oil
1 dried chipotle chile
2 cloves garlic, minced
2 teaspoons kosher salt
1 teaspoon ground cumin
1 teaspoon whole Mexican oregano
1½ tablespoons chopped cilantro or epazote

FINISH
2 tablespoons bacon drippings
4 cloves garlic, minced
1 white onion, minced
3 Roma tomatoes, chopped
1 jalapeño, minced
½ teaspoon Mexican oregano
⅓ cup 100% Agave Gold Tequila
2 cloves garlic, minced

GARNISH
Chopped cilantro
Chile tepins
Lime wedges
Chopped white onion

Sort beans, removing any foreign material, and rinse well. Place beans in a large, deep pan filled with water and 1 tablespoon white vinegar. Let beans soak overnight; remove from water, rinse well. Place beans, 6 cups fresh water, beer, bacon, diced onion, oil, chile, garlic, salt, cumin, and 1 teaspoon oregano in a large pot over medium-high heat and bring to a boil; reduce heat and simmer for a few hours until beans are tender. Use a potato masher to mush up just a few of the beans, enough to slightly thicken.

To finish, sauté the minced onion and garlic in the reserved bacon drippings in a skillet over medium heat for about 5 minutes or until lightly browned. Add Roma tomatoes, jalapeño, ½ teaspoon oregano, and tequila, and sauté for 5 minutes more. Add to pot of beans. Simmer for ½ hour more. Adjust seasoning. Serve with cilantro, chiles, lime, and onion on the side.

Serves 8 to 10.

cajun rice

The mandatory side dish for Blackened Swordfish.

2 cups converted rice
2½ cups chicken broth
1½ tablespoons unsalted butter, melted
1½ tablespoons finely chopped celery
1½ tablespoons finely chopped red bell pepper
1½ tablespoons finely chopped white onion
½ teaspoon salt
⅛ teaspoon cayenne pepper
⅛ teaspoon onion powder
⅛ teaspoon granulated garlic
⅛ teaspoon white pepper
⅛ teaspoon black pepper

In a small, covered baking dish, combine all ingredients, mix well, and cover with lid. Bake at 350° for about 1 hour and 10 minutes, or until rice is tender. Serve immediately.

Makes 8 to 10 servings.

grill-roasted baby vegetables

In the spring when the baby summer squash are in the market we always make this dish.

5 to 8 assorted baby vegetables per guest
Extra-virgin olive oil
Kosher salt

Place the vegetables in a large baking dish and lightly drizzle with olive oil, sprinkle salt over top, and indirectly grill-bake for 30 minutes in a grill preheated to 375°. Let cool 5 minutes and serve.

chile rellenos

When I want to see how a Mexican restaurant measures up, I order a Chile Relleno. Making a great one is the turning point in the life of a Southwestern cook.

15 whole poblano chiles
1½ pounds of your favorite cheese, cut
into ½ x ¾ x 2-inch chunks
(or whatever will fit inside chiles)
Flour for dredging chiles
8 eggs
½ teaspoon cream of tartar
Pinch of salt
Safflower oil for frying chiles

If you have access to hatch green chiles, use them—they are great—but I've had better results year-round with poblanos. Don't remove the stems. Blister the chiles on the grill until all of the outsides are brown and black. Place the chiles in a plastic or paper bag and fold the bag down. Let the chiles stand for 10 minutes and then peel them.

Put a chunk of cheese inside a small slit you've made in the side of each chile. Dredge the chiles in flour.

Separate the eggs and beat the yolks. In a large mixing bowl or food processor, beat the whites and ½ teaspoon cream of tarter with a pinch of salt until very stiff. Fold in the beaten yolks gently with a rubber spatula.

Meanwhile, in a large saucepan, heat safflower oil to at least 350°. Pick up one chile at a time by the stem, dip in the egg batter and very carefully (if you are not used to doing this, use tongs) set them in the hot oil. Chiles will float on top of the oil. Turn them carefully. When they are golden brown, they are done. Place them on paper towels to drain and salt them lightly.

Makes 15 chile rellenos.

opposite: *Chile Relleno (recipe above) with Ancho Chile Sauce (recipe page 67) and Avocado-Corn Salsa (recipe page 35), and in the bowls to the right, Avocado Tomatillo Salsa (recipe page 34), and Salsa de la Casa (recipe page 39).*

mango sesame rice

A great tropical side dish when everyday rice won't do!

1 fresh mango, cubed
2 tablespoons white sesame seeds
2 tablespoons mirin*
1½ cups sushi rice
2 cups vegetable broth

Mix all ingredients together and bring to a boil in a medium saucepan over medium heat. Reduce heat to low, cover, and simmer for 20 minutes. Remove from heat and let stand for 10 more minutes without lifting the lid.

Serves 6 to 8.

A sweetened sake available in the Asian food section of grocery stores.

confetti rice pilaf

This delicious side dish is almost too pretty to eat. . . . almost.

3½ cups vegetable broth, heated
1 teaspoon saffron threads
1 white onion, sliced thin
2 shallots, diced
3 cloves garlic, minced
⅓ cup extra-virgin olive oil
1½ cups long-grain rice
⅓ cup wild rice
6 ounces butternut squash, chopped
6 ounces carrots, julienned
1 yellow bell pepper, diced
5 plum tomatoes, peeled, seeded, and chopped
Salt and freshly ground black pepper to taste
Strips of yellow, orange, red, purple, and green bell pepper for garnish

Place ¼ cup of the hot vegetable broth in a small bowl and add the saffron. Let the saffron steep for at least 5 minutes.

Sauté the onion, shallots, and garlic in the oil for 3 minutes over medium heat. Add rices and toss until well coated with oil, about 2 minutes. Add the saffron mixture, the remaining broth, and squash. Stir while pilaf comes to a boil. Reduce heat to low and cover. Allow pilaf to cook, covered, for 15 minutes (set a timer). Add carrots, yellow bell, tomatoes, and salt and pepper, cook over low heat for 5 more minutes or until long-grain rice is tender. Top with strips of assorted bell peppers. Serve.

Serves 8.

mexican green rice

Nothing says Mexico like this simple, delicious side dish. It can be found on the tables of the ranches in northern Mexico. It's easy to make and you can add whatever touches you like.
It is especially good with fish and poultry.

1 ½ cups long-grain rice
¾ cup loosely packed, chopped
flat-leaf parsley
¾ cup loosely packed, chopped cilantro or
epazote
1 clove garlic, diced
2 (14½-ounce) cans chicken or
vegetable broth (homemade tastes better)
¼ cup safflower oil
2 Anaheim or poblano chiles, roasted,
peeled, and diced
(canned chiles will do in a pinch)
¼ cup white onion, chopped
1 small zucchini, diced
½ teaspoon salt

GARNISH
1 whole Anaheim or poblano chile, roasted,
peeled, and sliced into strips
1 red bell pepper, roasted, peeled and
sliced into strips

Soak the rice in a medium bowl of very hot water for 10 minutes. Drain the rice and rinse in cold water; let all excess water drain off. In a blender, process the parsley, cilantro or epazote, garlic, with one can of broth until smooth. Lightly brown the rice in the oil in a large frying pan over medium/medium-high heat. When rice is golden brown add the diced chiles and onion and continue cooking until onions are translucent. Stir often and do not let stick. Add broth mixture from blender and continue to cook for about 7 minutes, stirring often. Add zucchini, second can of broth and salt, and mix. As soon as the rice comes to a full boil, turn heat to low and cover for 20 minutes. Stir before serving. Garnish with strips of roasted chile.

Serves 6.

grilled corn on the cob with lime and chile

You'll never look at an ear of corn the same way again after trying it this way. It's an old Mexican treat.

Ears of fresh corn
Butter or vegetable-oil spray
Limes
Paprika
Salt

Boil corn until tender, about 6 minutes. Coat with butter or vegetable-oil spray. Grill over medium heat, allowing grill marks. Remove from heat, squeeze lime over corn, and sprinkle with paprika. Salt to taste.

habanero-lime butter

This condiment is out of this world on vegetables and potatoes, and you won't believe the flavor it gives grilled fish or pork.

½ cup sweet butter
1 habanero, minced
2 tablespoons fresh lime juice
2 cloves garlic
1 teaspoon salt
½ teaspoon dark brown sugar
Pinch of fresh black pepper

Whip all ingredients together in a blender or food processor. Roll into a log in waxed paper and chill.

opposite: *Grilled Shrimp Borracho with Sonoran Lime-Chipotle Marinade (recipe page 86) and Grilled Corn on the Cob with Lime and Chile (recipe above).*

mushroom-chipotle gravy

To give grill-roasted meats the perfect Sonoran twist, try this delicious gravy.

3 tablespoons butter
⅓ cup all-purpose flour
4 cups beef broth
Drippings from beef roast
Leaves from 4 sprigs of fresh thyme
Salt and pepper to taste
1 tablespoon chile powder made from:
1 chipotle chile, seeded and ground
1 ancho chile, seeded and ground
6 to 8 Italian brown mushrooms, sliced

Make a light brown roux from the butter and flour by whisking it constantly in a saucepan over medium heat. Pour the beef broth into the pan of drippings and de-glaze over medium heat. Slowly add to the roux, constantly whisking. Add the thyme, salt, pepper, and chile powder. Allow the mixture to simmer and reduce to desired thickness. Add mushrooms, stir in, and remove from heat. Allow to rest for 5 minutes before serving.

oysters rancheros

We don't need no stinking "Rockefeller."

12 fresh medium oysters in the shell
¼ pound Gorgonzola cheese, grated
Ranchero sauce, warm
1 bunch fresh cilantro, well washed
2 serrano chiles, sliced paper thin
Rock salt
Lemon wedges

Open the oysters and remove top half of the shell. Check for sand or grit and cut oyster loose from bottom shell, leaving oyster and liquid in the shell. Top each oyster with 2 teaspoons Gorgonzola. Place the oysters under the broiler and melt the cheese to golden brown. Remove from oven and spoon 1 teaspoon ranchero sauce across the center of the oyster, making a line of sauce down the middle. Place 3 cilantro leaves on one side of the line and 1 slice serrano chile on the other. Serve on a bed of rock salt with lemon wedges.

Serves 4.

north carolina coleslaw

This coleslaw is for topping North Carolina Pulled Pork sandwiches.

¾ head green cabbage, shredded
¼ head purple cabbage, shredded
3 carrots, grated
1½ cups heavy mayonnaise
½ cup white vinegar
⅓ cup sugar
1 tablespoons celery seeds
Salt and pepper to taste

Mix the cabbage and carrots together. Whisk together all other ingredients. Stir the dressing into the cabbage and mix well. Refrigerate before serving.

Makes enough for 8 to 10 sandwiches.

piñon-nut and fresh roasted green-chile stuffing

We always serve this delicious stuffing over the holidays with our turkey. My kids love it.

6 cups dry bread crumb cubes
⅓ cup finely chopped parsley
⅓ cup finely chopped white onion
2 teaspoons poultry seasoning
1 teaspoon salt
½ cup chopped celery
¾ cup shelled piñon nuts
3 to 5 fresh green chiles or ½ cup diced canned green chiles
(Fresh roasted chiles have a far better taste)
2 cups chicken or turkey broth

Combine bread crumbs, parsley, onion, poultry seasoning, salt, celery, piñon nuts, and ½ cup of the green chiles. Toss. Add broth slowly, stirring, and let stand until moistened. Stuff your turkey and roast as usual.

Makes 10 cups stuffing, or enough for a 14-pound turkey.

You may want to try adding piñon nuts and green chiles to your family recipe. If you do, I would suggest reducing the level of spices, because of the delicate flavor of the piñon nuts. Butter is not used in this recipe due to the natural oil in the piñon nuts.

yucca root with tangerine-grapefruit sauce

Yucca root is delicious and in this dish it's unbelievable!

1½ pounds yucca root
¼ cup extra-light olive oil
4 cloves garlic, minced
1 pink grapefruit, sectioned, skin and seeds removed, chopped into ¾-inch pieces
2 tangerines, sectioned, skin and seeds removed, chopped into ¾-inch pieces
¼ medium red onion, julienned
½ bunch chives, coarsely chopped
1 tablespoon Italian parsley, chopped
1 tablespoon cilantro, chopped
Juice of 1 lime
Salt

Bring 1½ gallons of salted water to a boil in a large pot. Peel and quarter yucca root, remove tough core, and cut into 2-inch pieces. Simmer yucca root for 45 minutes, until totally translucent. Allow yucca root to cool down in the cooking water to avoid hardening. Sauté garlic in olive oil over medium heat for about 2 minutes, until translucent, stirring occasionally. Remove pan from heat. Fold in grapefruit, tangerines, red onion, chives, parsley, cilantro, and lime juice. Salt to taste. Drain yucca root, place in serving bowl, and spoon sauce from pan over top.

Makes 4 cups.

summer bruschetta

Fresh toasted baguettes, good red wine, bruschetta, and someone you love. . . . life is good!

3 cups diced fresh plum tomatoes
1 loosely packed cup fresh basil, finely chopped
3 or 4 cloves garlic, run through a garlic press
1 teaspoon kosher salt
1 tablespoon extra-virgin olive oil
1 teaspoon balsamic vinegar

Mix ingredients together well; let stand 1/2 hour, serve, and enjoy.

Makes 3½ cups.

grill-baked scalloped potatoes

This simple side dish is a sure winner, especially with the kids! Think of it as Irish lasagna. It is layered about the same.

3 tablespoons melted butter
4½ cups thinly sliced white potatoes
1½ cups thinly sliced white onion
2 tablespoons all-purpose flour
¼ cup Italian parsley, chopped
Paprika
Salt
Freshly ground black pepper
1¾ cups milk
½ cup Cheddar cheese

Drizzle 1 teaspoon of the butter in the bottom of a medium baking dish. Spread the butter around (I use a potato slice).

Line the bottom of the pan with potato slices, then sprinkle some onion, a little flour, parsley, paprika, salt and pepper, and drizzle about 2 teaspoons butter over everything. Repeat this process until the dish is full.

Gently pour the milk in on the side, so you don't disturb the top layer. Light one side of the grill and place the dish on the other and close the lid. Check in about 45 minutes by poking center with a fork. If potatoes feel firm they need more cooking. When potatoes feel done, top with cheese. Wait about 5 minutes, depending on your grill temperature, allowing the cheese to melt. Remove from grill and allow to cool and blend for 10 minutes before serving.

Serves 6 to 8.

If until now your idea of barbecue

and grilling has been a piece of

meat covered with a store-bought barbecue sauce, then

barbecue

hold on to your hat. These rubs, sauces, and marinades

sauces and rubs

will take you to the next level of smoking, grilling, and

barbecuing. Be careful because after this chapter you'll be

grilling fish, poultry, and meats so full of flavor that your

family will refuse to go out for dinner!

rosemary dijon baste

This tangy basting sauce gives roasted lamb a wonderful tangy, fresh, light flavor.

1½ teaspoons fresh rosemary, minced
2 cloves garlic, minced or pressed
¼ cup peanut oil
2 tablespoons freshly squeezed
lemon juice
2 tablespoons Dijon mustard
1 tablespoon soy sauce
Pinch of salt

Whisk all ingredients well. Use to baste lamb while roasting.

Makes enough to baste 1 leg of lamb.

sonoran tamarind sauce

This sauce is wonderful on any roast pork.

¼ cup red wine vinegar
3 tablespoons dark brown sugar
2 cloves garlic, minced
1½ cups beef broth
⅓ cup tamarind paste
1 teaspoon grated ginger root

In a medium saucepan, bring vinegar, brown sugar, and garlic to a low boil, whisking until brown sugar has completely dissolved. Boil, stirring often until liquid has reduced by half; liquid will be a syrup at this point. Lower heat to a simmer and whisk in the beef broth. Whisk in the tamarind paste. Stir in the ginger and simmer to let sauce reduce a little more. Pour sauce through sieve into a serving bowl.

Spoon over sliced pork tenderloin.

Makes about 1 cup.

creole sauce

This sauce is great on just about anything, which pretty much sums up the Cajun diet.

SPICES
2 whole bay leaves
¾ teaspoon Greek oregano
¾ teaspoon cayenne pepper
¾ teaspoon Kosher salt
½ teaspoon Hungarian paprika
½ teaspoon white pepper
½ teaspoon dried basil
½ teaspoon ground thyme
½ teaspoon fresh ground black pepper

SAUCE
¼ cup sweet butter
½ cup minced red bell pepper
½ cup white minced onion
¾ cup minced celery
¼ cup minced shallots
¼ cup minced pablano chile
2 cloves garlic, minced
1¼ cups chicken broth
1 cup canned, peeled, and diced tomatoes
1 cup tomato sauce
1 teaspoon brown sugar
½ teaspoon Louisiana hot sauce

Mix spices together. In a large skillet over medium heat, melt the butter and sauté the spices, bell pepper, onion, celery, shallots pablano, and garlic for about 5 minutes or until onions are soft. Stir in all other ingredients, bring to boil, and reduce heat and simmer on low for about 20 minutes. Remove bay leaf before serving.

Makes 5 cups.

missouri basting sauce

If you love that Midwestern barbecue flavor, try my basting sauce for pork spare ribs: it makes them so tender!

1 ¾ cup white vinegar
2 tablespoons Tabasco Habanero Sauce
1 teaspoon kosher salt
1 teaspoon freshly ground black pepper
1 tablespoon dark brown sugar
1 teaspoon sugar

Mix all ingredients in a glass bowl and cover.

Baste pork while slow-smoking. This sauce will keep fresh in the refrigerator for 2 months.

Makes enough to baste 2 sections of ribs.

country-style pork rib rub

The use of nutmeg, marjoram, and mustard brings out the full flavor of these tender ribs.

5 tablespoons Hungarian paprika
5 tablespoons dark brown sugar
3 tablespoons kosher salt
2 tablespoons freshly ground, coarse
black pepper
1 tablespoon granulated garlic
1 tablespoon New Mexico mild chile powder
1 ½ teaspoons onion powder
1 teaspoon cayenne pepper
1 teaspoon marjoram
1 teaspoon mustard powder
½ teaspoon freshly ground nutmeg

Mix all ingredients together and store in a covered container. Rub well into Country-Style Pork Boneless Ribs before slow-smoking.

Makes enough to rub 2 racks of ribs.

opposite: *Pork spare ribs with Missouri Basting Sauce (recipe above) and Texas Barbecue Rub (recipe page 66).*

north carolina pulled-pork rub

This rub is for Eastern North Carolina Pulled-Pork Sandwiches (recipe page 77).

¼ cup New Mexico mild red chile powder
1 tablespoon dark brown sugar
1 tablespoon ground cumin
1 tablespoon kosher salt
1 tablespoon sugar
½ tablespoon freshly ground black pepper
1 teaspoon cayenne pepper

Mix all ingredients together well. Rub over roast, and allow roast to rest for 20 to 30 minutes before smoking.

Makes enough for 1 large pork shoulder.

eastern north carolina pulled-pork barbecue sauce

This sauce is for Eastern North Carolina Pulled-Pork Sandwiches, (page 74). There is also a Western North Carolina variety, which includes catsup, but for my money this is the best barbecue sandwich in all the South.

¾ cup white vinegar
2 tablespoons Louisiana Hot Sauce
1 tablespoon brown sugar
1 tablespoon sugar
1 tablespoon kosher salt
1 teaspoon crushed red pepper flakes
1 teaspoon freshly ground black pepper
½ teaspoon cayenne pepper

Whisk ingredients together well; add to roasted, chopped, or pulled pork, to taste.

Makes about 1¼ cups.

tequila grilling sauce for fish

Give grilled fish the flavors of the Sea of Cortés with this spicy grilling sauce.

3 tablespoons white tequila
3 tablespoons pineapple juice
2 tablespoons chopped cilantro
2 tablespoons fresh lime juice
2 tablespoons olive oil
2 cloves garlic, minced
1 habanero, minced
2 teaspoons kosher salt
½ teaspoon dark brown sugar
Pinch of freshly ground black pepper

Whisk ingredients together.

Rinse fish fillets under very cold water and dry with a paper towel.

Drizzle tequila sauce over fish while grilling.

Makes enough to grill four 6-ounce or two 8-ounce fish fillets.

mayan red recado marinade

This marinade gives fish or poultry a true Mayan flavor.

3 tablespoons Recado Colorado
(recipe page 69)
Juice of two Valencia oranges
Juice of two limes
Juice of one lemon
1 tablespoon orange zest
1 tablespoon lime zest
1 tablespoon lemon zest
¼ cup avacado oil
1 canned chipotle chile with 2 teaspoons
adobo sauce, mashed
½ bunch cilantro, chopped
1 teaspoon Mexican oregano

Whisk together lemon, lime, and orange juice and their zest. Slowly whisk in the avacado oil. Add all other ingredients and whisk well.

Makes about 1½ cups.

tri-tip marinade

This recipe is the one that I always cook for big parties, but it's great for small parties, too!

½ cup dark Mexican beer
½ cup basic vinaigrette
¾ cup soy sauce
4 chile tepins
3 cloves garlic, minced
1 teaspoon dark brown sugar
½ diced white onion
1 tablespoon white vinegar

Whisk all ingredients together and place in a large Tupperware or other covered, nonreactive bowl. Add tri-tip and marinate for at least 4 hours, turning every couple of hours. I usually marinate overnight.

Makes enough for 3 tri-tips.

asian beef marinade

This marinade gives grilled beef a wonderful Asian twist and works very well with tri-tip or London broil.

¾ cup soy sauce
½ cup Sapporo Black Stout Draft
1 tablespoon safflower oil
1 tablespoon sesame oil
2 Thai chiles, chopped
3 cloves garlic, minced
2 teaspoons sugar
1½ tablespoons seasoned rice vinegar

Purée all ingredients together in a blender or food processor and place in a large Tupperware or other covered, nonreactive bowl. Marinate for at least 4 hours, turning every couple of hours. I usually marinate overnight.

Makes 1½ cups.

sonoran brisket rub

Try giving your next smoked brisket a Sonoran flavor.

¼ cup Hungarian paprika
3 tablespoons brown sugar
1 ground chipotle chile, with seeds
2 tablespoons freshly ground black pepper
2 tablespoons ground cumin
2 tablespoons kosher salt
1 tablespoon New Mexico mild red
chile powder
1 tablespoon granulated garlic
1 teaspoon Mexican oregano

Mix and store in a covered container. Rub brisket well before slow-smoking.

Makes enough to rub 1 whole brisket.

sonoran brisket marinade

This marinade is quick and easy. I find it best to let brisket marinate overnight in the refrigerator. As always, add your own touches.

¼ cup basic vinaigrette
¾ cup soy sauce
¼ cup dark Mexican beer
½ teaspoon crushed red pepper
2 cloves garlic, minced
1 teaspoon dark brown sugar
½ diced white onion

Place brisket in a large Tupperware or other covered bowl. Whisk all remaining ingredients together and place in bowl. Marinate for at least 4 hours, turning every couple of hours.

Makes 1½ cups

ruby prickly pear–red chile glaze

Wow your friends with this treat from the Sonoran Desert. I use it on Cornish rock game hens. It works well on any poultry.

½ cup red chile jelly
2 tablespoons prickly-pear syrup

Thin red chile jelly with prickly-pear syrup. Baste a roasting hen with glaze in last 10 minutes. Keep your eye on this; it has a tendency to burn due to the sugar.

Makes ½ cup.

apricot-pecan poultry glaze

So you've tried barbecue sauce and you're ready for something different. This glaze gives chicken a new dimension, not to mention makes the cook look like a pro just out of cooking school.

½ cup apricot jelly or preserves
¼ cup water
¼ cup whole pecans

In a small saucepan, whisk together the jelly and water and bring to a boil. Add the pecans, stir in, and let cool. If using on the grill, spoon over chicken or fish in the last 10 minutes, as the sugar will burn.

Makes 1 cup.

opposite: *Whole chicken with Ruby Prickly Pear–Red Chile Glaze and whole chicken with Apricot-Pecan Poultry Glaze (both recipes above).*

texas barbecue rub

Okay, so you want to learn about smoking meats. This is where you start. Try using a rub like this one in place of barbecue sauce. It will enhance the flavor of good, slow-smoked meat.

5 tablespoons Hungarian paprika
3 tablespoons dark brown sugar
1½ tablespoons ground chile de arbol
1 tablespoon New Mexico mild red
chile powder
2 tablespoons freshly ground coarse
black pepper
2 tablespoons ground cumin
2 tablespoons kosher salt
1 tablespoon sugar

Mix ingredients together and store in a covered container. Rub well onto brisket, clod, or ribs before slow-smoking.

Makes 1 cup.

chunky cranberry-jalapeño dipping sauce

Try this unexpected sauce with fish or foul.

1 pound fresh cranberries, washed
and sorted
½ cup sherry vinegar
¼ cup key lime juice
1 cup dark brown sugar
1 jalapeño, chopped
2 teaspoons ground cinnamon
½ teaspoon allspice
½ teaspoon ground cloves
½ teaspoon Hungarian paprika
½ teaspoon kosher salt

Run cranberries through a food processor until coarsely chopped. Place all ingredients in a medium saucepan and simmer for 15 minutes. Allow to cool.

Makes 2½ cups.

western barbecue sauce

Forget store-bought barbecue sauce, this is the real enchilada.

1½ tablespoons safflower oil
2 large white onions, chopped
2 (14-ounce) cans crushed tomatoes
1 (14-ounce) can tomato sauce
1 (14-ounce) can tomato purée
1¼ cups white vinegar
½ cup freshly squeezed orange juice
¼ cup Dijon mustard
2 tablespoons molasses
1 tablespoon liquid smoke
1 clove garlic, minced
2 tablespoons sugar
2 tablespoons dark brown sugar
1 tablespoon salt
1 tablespoon freshly ground black pepper
1 teaspoon Mexican oregano
1 tablespoon mild New Mexico red chile powder
1 tablespoon Hungarian paprika
½ teaspoon ground cayenne pepper

In a stock pot, brown the onions in the oil. Add all ingredients and bring to a full boil. Reduce heat to low and lightly simmer for at least 4 hours. Keep an eye on it to keep it from sticking. When sauce is done, run it through your blender a little at a time until it's all smooth. Will keep in the refrigerator for up to 2 weeks.

Makes about ½ gallon.

ancho chile sauce

A must with chile rellenos!

3 dried ancho chiles
1¾ cups chicken broth
1 clove minced garlic
½ teaspoon ground cumin
½ teaspoon kosher salt

Roast the chiles on a hot comal until soft and pliable. Remove chiles from comal and allow to cool down a little. Remove stems and seeds. Place all ingredients in a sauce pan and simmer for 15 minutes. Pour in a blender and purée. Pour the sauce through a sieve into a bowl, mash with the back of a spoon, until chile solids are left. Discard chile solids. Serve warm.

Makes about 1½ cups.

citrus peanut sauce

If you really want to be a local hero at the grill, sooner or later you're going to have to try grilled fruit. This sauce really makes it shine!

½ cup chunky peanut butter
¼ cup lime juice
3 tablespoons freshly squeezed orange juice
2 tablespoons dark Jamaican rum
1 tablespoon honey
1 teaspoon ground cinnamon
½ teaspoon white pepper

Combine all ingredients in a blender. Brush fruit before grilling.

Makes 1 cup.

habanero and dark jamaican rum barbecue sauce

Serve this very spicy, tropical sauce on the side with slow-smoked pork or poultry.

2 tablespoons safflower oil
2 large white onions, peeled and diced
2 tablespoons fresh ginger, grated
5 cloves fresh garlic, minced
1 cup Meyers Dark Jamaican Rum
1 cup catsup
½ cup red wine vinegar
½ cup dark molasses
¼ cup dark brown sugar
½ habanero pepper, seeded and minced
1 tablespoon ground allspice
Pinch of mace
Salt and pepper to taste

In a medium saucepan, sauté the onions in hot oil until translucent. Add the ginger and garlic and sauté for about 1 minute more to allow flavors to blend. Add the rum (remember: rum is flammable!), catsup, vinegar, molasses, brown sugar, habanero, allspice, and mace. Bring to a full boil, reduce heat, and simmer for ½ hour. Remove from heat, season with salt and pepper, and allow to cool.

Makes about 4.

recado colorado

Try this Mayan spice paste on meat, fowl or fish. It's also great in soup or stews.

1 large white onion, grill toasted
2 bulbs garlic, grill toasted
1½ inch piece cinnamon stick
2 Tbl. assorted peppercorns
2 Tbl. Achiote Rojo (Spiced seasoning paste)
1½ tsp. Mexican oregano
10 cloves
½ tsp. ground allspice
¼ tsp. ground cumin

Place the onion and garlic on the grill and slowly toast the outsides.

Remove from the grill and allow to cool.

Place all other ingredients in a spice grinder (or well cleaned coffee grinder).

Grind into a fine powder.

Remove the peel from the onion and garlic. Roughly chop the onion and place the onion and garlic an a blender. puree. Add the spices and puree until well blended. Store in the refrigerator in an air tight container.

spicy asian kumquat sauce

For duck and other poultry.

5 kumquats, sliced into rounds
3 tablespoons sugar
⅓ cup seasoned rice vinegar
3 tablespoons grenadine
¾ cups orange juice
2 teaspoons soy juice
1 tablespoon freshly squeezed lime juice
1 teaspoon freshly squeezed lemon juice
2 teaspoons dried cherries, minced
½ teaspoon kosher salt
½ teaspoon white pepper
1 Thai chile, topped
5 fresh basil leaves minced

In a saucepan over medium-low heat, simmer the kumquats, sugar, vinegar, grenadine, orange juice, and soy sauce, and reduce by about half, 10 to 12 minutes. Remove from heat and whisk in lime juice, cherries, salt, pepper, and chile. Carefully stir in basil. This sauce goes on the duck just before serving. Enjoy!

Makes about ¾ cups.

When we hear the words "grilling"

or "barbecue," the first image that

comes into most of our minds is of a big piece of juicy

main dishes

meat slow roasting over a smoky fire. In this chapter, we

get to the heart of Sonoran grilling with dishes like

Sonoran Mesquite-Smoked Brisket, Herbed Spit-Roasted

Leg of Lamb, and Grill-Roasted Habanero Pork Tenderloin

with Sonoran Tamarind Sauce. As always, follow these

easy recipes and soon you'll be grilling like a pro!

pork (and a little lamb)

Pork is at the center of many fantastic Mexican dinners. Some folks say pork is the other white meat, but down here, we say it's the only white meat! You'll also find a great recipe for leg of lamb (that beautiful one on the cover).

grilled chinese-style barbecued pork ribs

Traditionally, Chinese-style pork ribs are deep fried. I find these slow-smoked ribs less greasy and much more flavorful.

MARINADE
¾ cup grenadine
½ cup soy sauce
¼ cup dry sherry
¼ cup plum sauce
¼ cup minced green onions
3 tablespoons rice vinegar
4 cloves garlic, minced
2 tablespoons grated fresh ginger
2 tablespoons sugar
2 teaspoons peanut oil
½ teaspoon freshly ground black pepper

6 pounds of pork ribs

Combine all marinade ingredients. Marinate ribs overnight and reserve a little extra marinade for brushing during slow smoking.*

Serves 5 to 10 people, depending on appetite.

Remember that the trick with pork ribs is to indirectly smoke them at about 190° to 200°, the longer the better. Meat should contract and pull away from the bone easily, and be fully cooked all the way through the center.

grill-roasted pork chops with sonoran-herbed mushroom stuffing

You won't believe how juicy pork chops are when grilled over green onions.

½ ounce dried morel mushrooms
2 (1-pound) loaves soft French bread,
crusts removed
1½ white onions, diced
3 shallots, diced
4 stalks celery, diced, reserving ¼ cup
of the leaves
½ cup sweet butter
3 cups assorted fresh mushrooms, rinsed
and chopped
1 cup chicken broth
3 eggs, lightly beaten
4 roasted poblanos, chopped
¼ cup Italian parsley, finely chopped
2 teaspoons finely chopped tarragon
1 teaspoon finely chopped sage
2 teaspoons brown sugar
½ teaspoon freshly ground nutmeg
Kosher salt
Freshly ground black pepper
4 thick-cut pork chops
2 bunches green onions

Rinse the dried mushrooms and soak in 2 cups hot water, covered with plastic, for 25 minutes. Remove with a slotted spoon, roughly chop, and place back in liquid. Set aside.

While mushrooms are soaking, tear the bread into ¾- to 1-inch pieces, place on a cookie sheet and lightly bake in the grill for 15 minutes to dry out. Remove dried bread from grill and raise heat to 350°.

In a large skillet over medium heat, sauté the onions, shallots, and celery (without leaves) in butter until onions and celery are soft, about 10 to 15 minutes. Add morels with liquid, fresh mushrooms, and chicken broth. Sauté, stirring often, until mixture is almost dry. Remove from heat and allow to cool.

Combine bread, eggs, celery leaves, chiles, fresh herbs, brown sugar, and nutmeg in a large bowl; stir well. Stir in cooked mushroom mixture and add salt and pepper to taste. Spoon into a cavity cut into the side of each pork chop and grill over a bed of green onions until chops are browned on the outside and centers are 165°.

Serves 4.

grilled pork chop with guajillo chile sauce

Guajillo chiles have a slightly sweet flavor that goes well with grill-roasted pork!

15 dried guajillo chiles
3 cups beef broth
3 cloves garlic, minced
2 teaspoons dark brown sugar
1 teaspoon Mexican oregano
½ teaspoon ground cumin
½ teaspoon kosher salt
6 thick cut pork chops

Roast the chiles on a hot comal until soft and pliable. Remove chiles from comal and allow to cool down a little. Remove stems and seeds. Place all ingredients in a sauce pan and simmer for 15 minutes. Pour in a blender, ¾ of a cup at a time, and purée (Be careful, hot liquids expand in a blender and can spill out the top and burn you). Pour the sauce through a sieve into a bowl, mash with the back of a spoon, until chile solids are left. Discard chile solids. If sauce is too thin, return to heat and thicken. Serve warm, with any grilled pork.

Makes enough for 6 thick-cut pork chops.

The trick to juicy pork chops is not to overcook them. Using a meat thermometer, cook until internal temperature is 165° at the thickest part of the chop.

opposite: *Grilled Pork Chop with Guajillo Chile Sauce (recipe above) and Mexican Green Rice (recipe page 47).*

grill-roasted habanero pork tenderloin

Succulent, spicy, and savory, this juicy pork tenderloin is always a big winner in my kitchen.

3 (8- to 10-ounce) pork tenderloins
1 cinnamon stick, crushed
1 teaspoon allspice
1 whole nutmeg, crushed
1 habanero chile, seeded
¾ cup chopped white onion
1½ cups chopped scallions, white part only
¾ cup shallots
⅓ cup fresh thyme
1½ tablespoons roughly chopped ginger root
¼ teaspoon balsamic vinegar
1 cup freshly squeezed orange juice
¾ cup olive oil
1 tablespoon soy sauce
½ teaspoon kosher salt
Pinch freshly ground black pepper
½ teaspoon dark brown sugar

Remove exterior skin and any excess fat from tenderloins. Place tenderloins in a large uncovered baking dish. Lightly brown cinnamon, allspice, and nutmeg over low heat in a small skillet. When spices have released their fragrance, place in a spice grinder and grind to a fine powder.

Place chile, onions, scallions, shallots, ground spices, thyme, and ginger in a food processor and process until finely chopped. While food processor is still running add balsamic vinegar, orange juice, 2 tablespoons olive oil, soy sauce, salt, pepper, and brown sugar.

Pour mixture from food processor over pork tenderloins. Cover with plastic wrap. Marinate for 4 to 6 hours, turning often.

Remove pork tenderloin from marinade and brush with remaining olive oil. Grill over mesquite charcoal for 15 to 20 minutes, turning and basting often. Pork is done when internal temperature reaches 165°. When done, slice and serve topped with Sonoran Tamarind Sauce (recipe page 56).

Serves 8 to 10.

country-style boneless pork ribs smoked in a stove-top smoker

I just love how juicy ribs come out in a Stove-Top Smoker. You simply must have one.

Country-Style Pork Rib Rub
(recipe page 58)
4 pounds pork ribs

Rub ribs well with ½ of the Country-Style Pork Rib Rub. Place dry wood grains in the bottom of the smoker pan. Place drip pan above wood grains and rack above drip pan. Place ribs in pan and close. Place on grill over one burner set on lowest setting and slow-cook for at least 1½ hours. Remove ribs from pan and pour drippings and remaining Country-Style Pork Rib Rub into a mixing bowl. Turn grill to high and roll ribs in dripping mixture to coat. Place ribs on grill over high heat and sear the outside.

Serves 8.

eastern north carolina pulled-pork barbecue sandwiches

People who know barbecue will tell you that this is the best barbecued pork sandwich in the world; I agree.

1 (4- to 5-pound) boneless pork butt
½ cup North Carolina Pulled-Pork Rub
(recipe page 60)
1 cup North Carolina Pulled-Pork Barbecue
Sauce (recipe page 60)
North Carolina Coleslaw (recipe page 51)
White hamburger buns

Rub all sides of the pork roast well with North Carolina Pulled-Pork Rub. Slow-smoke the roast until the meat is very tender and reaches an internal temperature of 165 to 170°. Remove from smoker, chop or shred the roast, mix in the Eastern North Carolina Pulled-Pork Barbecue Sauce and pile the meat on the hamburger buns. Top with North Carolina Coleslaw. Serve with a bottle of your favorite hot sauce and plenty of ice-cold beer.

Makes 15 to 20 sandwiches.

whole slow-smoked suckling pig with citrus-chile negro marinade

Try a Sonoran luau the next time you're having a big party around the pool.

MARINADE
2½ cups freshly squeezed orange juice
1 bottle Red Stripe Beer
2 cups Key lime juice
4 cups chopped cilantro
¼ cup dark brown sugar
3 chile negro, toasted lightly, stem and
seeds removed, and ground
20 cloves garlic, minced
½ cup minced fresh oregano leaves
¼ cup ground cumin
¼ cup Italian parsley
5 tablespoons kosher salt

1 whole suckling pig, split and washed
(12 to 15 pounds)

Combine all marinade ingredients.

Place the pig in a large pan and rub with marinade thoroughly. Keep pig in the refrigerator overnight, turning and basting every few hours.

Prop pig's mouth open with aluminum foil. Also cover ears and tail with aluminum foil. Reserve marinade for basting. Baste every 20 to 30 minutes. Stop basting in last hour of cooking and discard remaining marinade.

Slow-roast pig until internal temperature reads 160°, about 4 to 5 hours.

Serves 20.

green chile with pork

Homemade green chile is so wonderful. It's everything foods here in the Sonoran Desert are all about. And every good Sonoran cook should have at least one great green chile recipe in their bag of tricks. Most of us have had green chile burros. What about trying green chile as a main dish served with fresh corn bread?

2 pounds lean pork roast cut into
½-inch cubes
1 white onion, chopped
4 medium white potatoes, cut into
½-inch cubes
Lard or cooking oil for browning pork
1 (14-ounce) can diced tomatoes, drained
4 medium zucchini, chopped into
½-inch cubes
1½ pounds chopped green chiles
(I prefer fresh-roasted)
1 clove fresh garlic, minced
1 (48-ounce) can chicken broth
Salt to taste

In a large, heavy, lightly oiled skillet, brown the pork, onions, and potatoes. When brown, drain off any excess grease. Add tomatoes, zucchini, green chiles, garlic, and chicken broth. Salt to taste. Bring to a boil and simmer for about 1 hour. If stew gets too thick, add a little water. If too thin, add a little masa flour made into a paste. Stir often to prevent sticking.

Serves 8.

herbed spit-roasted leg of lamb

On that special night, with those special friends, tie it all together with a succulent, juicy leg of lamb slow-roasting over hot coals.

MARINADE
½ cup pinot grigio
½ cup olive oil
8 cloves garlic, chopped
Juice of three lemons
1 bunch of mint, cleaned and chopped
1 teaspoon kosher salt
Freshly ground black pepper
1 white onion, minced

1 (8-pound) leg of lamb, deboned and tied
Fresh rosemary for garnish

Whisk all marinade ingredients together. Pour into a large, food-grade plastic bag and add lamb. Tie closed and rub in the marinade (you may also do this in a large baking dish). Allow the lamb to rest in the marinade for 1½ hours.

Place lamb on spit and roast, indirectly, over medium-hot coals until internal temperature reaches 140° (for medium rare), or about 35 to 40 minutes. Remove lamb from spit and allow to rest for 8 to 10 minutes before serving. Garnish with rosemary.

Serves more people than you're willing to have over.

opposite: *Herbed Spit-Roasted Leg of Lamb (recipe above) with Rosemary Dijon Baste (recipe page 56).*

seafood

When the average person thinks about the Sonoran Desert they don't think about seafood. But Mexico has some of the best seafood in the world. I'll put my Grill-Roasted Sonoran Sea Bass, Oyster Rancheros, or Tequila-Grilled Orange Roughy Tacos up against the very best that the Delta, Seattle, Maine or anywhere else has to offer.

Imagine sitting under a cabana with your bare feet in the white sand. It's sunset and you're bathing in the fresh scent of the warm sea air coming in over the Sea of Cortés. From the little fish taco stand you watch the boats come and go, while eating shrimp tacos that were made about two minutes ago from shrimp that were caught this morning. They are served with a fiery, fresh, seafood salsa and a Mexican beer so cold it almost hurts your teeth. Elegant dining? No, something much more wonderful!

mesquite-seared ahi tuna steaks

These delicious steaks go well with a Baby Spinach Salad (recipe page 21) and Soy-Ginger Vinaigrette (recipe page 31).

#1 sushi-grade ahi tuna steaks
Sesame oil for brushing tuna steaks
Salt and pepper to taste

Brush tuna with sesame oil and salt and pepper on each side. Quickly sear both sides over hot mesquite charcoal, about 1 to 1½ minutes per side. Serve with Japanese soy sauce and wasabi.

Figure 4 to 5 ounces of ahi tuna per guest.

cherry & mesquite cold-smoked, reserva de la familia tequila-cured salmon

Try this delicious twist on smoked salmon. It's easier than you think, and so delicious!

2 large salmon fillets
1½ pounds dark brown sugar
1½ pounds kosher salt
½ cup Jose Quervo Reserva de la Familia Tequila (Other tequilas do not have the rich flavor of this fine tequila, and will not work well in this recipe. However, brandy may be substituted.)

Scale the fillets (this step is optional). Remove any finger bones and cut at least six 1-inch long holes in the skin to allow penetration of the brine. Place salmon in a baking dish, skin side down. Mix sugar and salt well and spread over the salmon. Drizzle tequila over salmon. Place a second baking dish (same size as the salmon dish) on top of the salmon and place approximately 6 pounds of weight in the upper dish (I use the family dictionary.) Set both dishes on a baking sheet to catch drippings, and let cure in the refrigerator for 24 hours. Remove from refrigerator and turn salmon over, placing weighted pan back on top, and let cure for 12 more hours. Remove from refrigerator, rinse well, dry with paper towel, and place in clean baking dish. Cover with plastic wrap and refrigerate 1 more day.

In a two-chamber smoker, light 2 to 3 pieces of pure mesquite charcoal in the fire box and start soaking cherry wood chips. In upper chamber, place large plastic tub or baking dish full of ice as far away from fire box as possible. Place salmon on sheet pan and set the pan on top of the ice. Use small butter dishes as spacers and place second sheet pan on top of the first. Do not allow top pan to touch salmon. Fill second sheet pan with ice. The idea is that you allow a very thin corridor for the salmon to lie in with ice both above and below. It is important that the salmon stay very cold; it is also important that just a few coals are used at a time. Add a few cherry wood chips at a time and smoke for 4 to 6 hours. Check on your ice and drain off excess water, adding more ice as necessary. Do not allow salmon to get wet.

When salmon is done smoking, lightly brush with olive oil. Serve sliced paper thin. Seal the salmon and refrigerate. Date sealed salmon; it will remain fresh for about two and a half weeks.

Makes enough for a very large brunch.

cedar plank-roasted fillet of salmon

Your local building supplier most likely has cedar planks. Measure your grill and have them cut the planks to fit. Make sure you choose a clean piece without knots.

1 cedar plank
4 to 5 cups pinot noir
¼ cup light olive oil
Squeeze of lemon
Salt and freshly ground black pepper to taste
5 sprigs thyme
5 sprigs rosemary
5 sprigs marjoram
1 salmon fillet
(keep in mind how big your cedar plank is)
Fresh dill, finely chopped
Lemon wedges for garnish
Chunky Cranberry-Jalapeño Dipping Sauce
(recipe page 66)

Place the plank in a container, or plastic food bag, large enough to totally immerse. Add a cup or two of pinot noir and fill to cover with water. Soak over night.

Forty-five minutes before grilling, whisk together 1½ cups water, 1½ cups pinot noir, ¼ cup olive oil, a squeeze of lemon, salt and pepper, and 1 sprig each of thyme, rosemary, and marjoram, in a glass bowl. Rinse salmon fillet under cold water, dry with paper towel, and add to marinade; cover with plastic and let stand. Light the grill about 10 minutes before grilling, turning on all burners. Remove plank from pinot bath, reserving liquid to control flame (see below).

Remove salmon from marinade and center on plank. Top with salt and pepper, 2 sprigs each of thyme, rosemary, and marjoram. Place on grill and turn off burners directly below plank, leaving indirect burners on high to medium setting (depending on your grill, you may leave burner below plank on lowest setting: about 350° to 400°). Close lid on grill. Keep an eye on the grill to avoid fires. If one occurs, simply drizzle pinot bath over flames, taking care not to burn yourself with steam. Grill salmon for 25 to 30 minutes. Salmon should be lightly opaque at center but still juicy. Remove from grill using an oven mitt. Remove herbs, top with Chunky Cranberry-Jalapeño Dipping Sauce to your liking, and garnish with thinly sliced lemon, 2 sprigs each of thyme, rosemary, and marjoram, and sprinkle lightly with chopped dill. Serve on plank with fresh baguette and lemon wedges.

Figure 4 to 5 ounces of salmon per guest.

grilled coconut shrimp

Light, delicious, and so tropical!

1 pound shell-on shrimp, uncooked
2/3 cup coconut milk
(canned, sweetened)
Juice of 1 lime
2 cloves garlic, crushed
1/2 medium jalapeño, chopped
2 teaspoons ground cumin
1 teaspoon ground coriander
1/2 teaspoon ground white pepper
1/2 teaspoon salt
12 to 18 fresh pineapple chunks
Vegetable spray
Shredded meat of coconut, at least 1/4 cup

Peel and devein shrimp. Combine coconut milk, lime juice, garlic, jalapeño, cumin, coriander, white pepper, and salt. Marinate no more than 1 hour.

Soak bamboo skewers in water for 20 minutes. Thread shrimp and pineapple chunks on skewers. Spray skewers with vegetable spray and grill 3 minutes per side, or until shrimp are done. Sprinkle coconut on skewers in last 1 minute of grilling.

Serves 4.

mayan sea scallops

Try these easy, delicious scallops.

1 pound sea scallops
Mayan Red Recado Marinade (recipe page 61)

Marinate the scallops for 4 hours and then grill until centers are white and no longer translucent (about 3 to 4 minutes per side). The first time you turn the scallops, drizzle with the marinade. If scallops start to shrink dramatically, they are being overcooked.

Serves 4.

grilled shrimp borracho with sonoran lime-chipotle marinade

Borracho means "drunken." The use of dark Mexican beer gives these spicy little devils a subtle, sweet flavor. This marinade also works very well with chicken or fish!

1 to 2 pounds jumbo shrimp, peeled
and deveined

MARINADE
(If making a large batch, double
marinade recipe)
Juice of 4 Key limes
½ cup dark Mexican beer
1 tablespoon extra-virgin olive oil
3 canned chipotle chiles, mashed well
¼ teaspoon kosher salt
2 cloves minced garlic
½ teaspoon Mexican oregano

Whisk all marinade ingredients together and brush over shrimp while grilling. Grill shrimp until they are no longer translucent at center. Shrimp should be nice and warm, but do not overgrill as this will cause them to be tough. Enjoy!

Serves 6.

crawfish étouffée

I love this spicy Cajun dish. Make sure you ask for domestic crawfish as they are much sweeter than the imported variety.

7 tablespoons safflower oil
¾ cup all-purpose flour
¼ cup poblano chile, seeded, veined, and chopped
¼ cup red bell pepper, chopped
¼ cup white onion, chopped
¼ cup celery, chopped
3 cups lobster, crawfish, or fish stock
1 cup green onions, chopped fine
3 pounds peeled crawfish tails
1 stick unsalted butter
4 cups Cajun Rice (recipe page 43)

ÉTOUFFÉE SPICE MIX
Mix together:
2 teaspoons cayenne pepper
2 teaspoons kosher salt
1 teaspoon dried basil
1 teaspoon white pepper
½ teaspoon dried thyme
½ teaspoon black pepper

In a large, heavy iron skillet, heat the oil over medium-high heat until hot. With a long-handled whisk, carefully whisk in the flour a little at a time until smooth. Keep whisking constantly, until roux is a dark red-brown, about 3 to 5 minutes. Do not let burn. Remove from heat. With a wooden spoon, stir in poblano chile, red bell, white onion, celery, and about half of the étouffée spice mix. Continue to stir until skillet cools down, about 4 to 5 minutes.

In a medium saucepan, over medium heat, bring 2 cups of the stock to a boil. Add the roux mixture and whisk constantly until roux is totally dissolved. Do not let burn. Remove from heat, and set aside.

In a large saucepan, over medium heat, sauté the green onions and crawfish in the butter for about 1 minute. Add remaining stock and roux mixture. Shake pan back and forth to mix flavors until butter is totally melted; stir gently if needed. Add remaining étouffée spice, stir well, and serve ¾ cup étouffée over ½ cup Cajun Rice. If sauce separates a little, add 1 or 2 tablespoons water or stock and shake pan until it binds.

Serves 8.

grill-roasted sea bass with serrano-orange tequila sauce

This grilled fish with Habanero-Lime Butter on the side is an absolute wonder. The flavor is unbelievable!

MARINADE

½ cup freshly squeezed orange juice

¼ cup safflower oil

3 tablespoons lime juice

1 tablespoon white tequila

3 serrano chiles, finely minced

1 teaspoon dark brown sugar

½ teaspoon paprika

Pinch allspice

Zest of 1 lime

1 clove garlic, minced

4 (6- to 8-ounce) sea bass fillets

Whisk all ingredients for marinade together in a large glass bowl.

Marinate fish for 3 hours, turning often. Grill over mesquite charcoal until fish is done. Serve with Habanero-Lime Butter (recipe page 49).

Serves 4.

opposite: *Grill-Roasted Sea Bass with Serrano-Orange Tequilla Sauce (recipe above).*

arizona fresh-water prawn scampi

If you can find the prawns that are farm-raised here in Arizona, use them; they are sweeter than regular prawns. But either way, this is one great scampi!

24 fresh-water prawns (unpeeled)
1 lemon
½ cup extra-virgin olive oil
8 cloves garlic, minced
1 teaspoon crushed red pepper
¼ teaspoon dried basil
¼ teaspoon dried chervil
¼ teaspoon dried, ground thyme
Salt and freshly ground black pepper to taste
1 cup pinot grigio
2 tablespoons butter
2 tablespoons Italian parsley, finely chopped, for garnish

Rinse the prawns well. Using a sharp knife, slice through the shell of the prawns along the back, but do not cut in half. Squeeze the lemon over the prawns and rub the juice in. Heat the oil in a large sauté pan over medium heat. Add the shrimp, turn up the heat a little, and sauté for 3 to 4 minutes until the prawns are pink. Add garlic, red pepper, spices, and salt and pepper. Stir well. Remove prawns to serving plate. Deglaze pan with white wine. Reduce wine sauce by half over high heat (about 1 minute). Remove from heat and stir in butter. Spoon wine sauce over prawns and garnish with parsley.

Serves 5 or 6.

grill-baked paella

If you want to know about Sonoran foods, you need to look at Spanish foods. This beautiful dish is a wonderful representation of that Spanish tradition.

½ cut-up fryer chicken
½ pound Italian rope sausage, spicy
1½ cups Italian arborio rice
2 tablespoons butter
1 tablespoon lobster base
3 cups boiling water
1 teaspoon saffron threads
1½ cups frozen baby peas, thawed
¼ cup Italian parsley, chopped
1 red bell pepper, diced
2 or 3 medium Italian brown
mushrooms, sliced
4 cloves garlic, minced
2 dashes of Louisiana Hot Sauce
2 teaspoons kosher salt
Freshly ground black pepper to taste
½- to ¾-pound assortment of shellfish
such as clams, mussels, cockles, and crab
claws: whatever is fresh
(I would not use oysters)
½ pound medium shrimp, peeled
1 lemon, cut in half

Place pizza stone on grill, light burners, and turn to low. Allow grill to slowly heat up to about 400°, and adjust heat to maintain 400°.

Place the chicken and sausage on the grill directly over heat and roast. Remove from grill, set aside. Place the rice, butter, and lobster base in a large, heavy baking dish with a heavy lid, pour the water in, and stir. Add saffron, peas, parsley, bell pepper, mushrooms, garlic, Louisiana Hot Sauce, salt, and pepper; stir well. Bake for 15 minutes; remove lid.

Place shell fish on top of mixture. Slice sausage, arrange roasted chicken and sausage in with rice and seafood, and cover. Place baking dish on pizza stone and grill-bake for 15 minutes or until shellfish and rice are completely done. Remove lid and squeeze 1 whole lemon over dish. Serve with a good cream sherry.

Serves the whole gang.

grill-roasted red snapper veracruz

Light the grill and crack open an ice-cold Mexican beer. This grilled snapper is not only spicy, light, and delicious, it's also a feast for the eyes!

2 (1½-pounds) whole red snapper,
cleaned and scaled
1 lemon, cut into quarters
Kosher salt
Freshly ground black pepper
2 plum tomatoes, sliced
1 shallot, sliced
2 Key limes, sliced
1 lemon, sliced
1 roasted poblano chile, cut into strips
2 cloves garlic, sliced
3 sprigs fresh cilantro
3 sprigs fresh thyme
3 fresh bay leaves
Extra-virgin olive oil to taste
Capers to taste

Place pizza stone on grill, light burners, and turn to low. Place wire rack with legs on pizza stone or use spacers to separate rack from hot stone. Allow grill to slowly heat up to about 450°, turn off burners directly below pizza stone, and adjust heat to maintain approximately 450°.

Rub the cleaned and scaled fish inside and out with lemon, and place in a baking dish. Season the fish cavities with salt and pepper, then place a little of all the ingredients, except the olive oil and capers, inside the fish. Scatter the remaining ingredients over the fish and in the baking dish, drizzle with a little olive oil, and season with salt and pepper.

Grill-roast the fish for about 20 to 30 minutes, or until skin is crisp and flesh is fully cooked. Allow to rest a few minutes before serving. Sprinkle a few capers over the fish before serving.

Serves 6.

tequila-grilled orange roughy tacos

Along the beach at the Sea of Cortés in Mexico, the fish tacos are rarely served this way. But I just love these wonderful tacos with a little lettuce and cheese. The taste is light, fresh, and delicious!

MARINADE
½ cup basil leaves, finely chopped
3 tablespoons white tequila
3 tablespoons freshly squeezed lime juice
2 tablespoons minced shallots
2 tablespoons avocado oil
1 tablespoon Mandarin Napoleon
(Grand Marnier will do)
2 teaspoons orange zest
2 teaspoons ground coriander
1 teaspoon lime zest
½ teaspoon freshly ground black pepper
½ teaspoon cayenne pepper
½ teaspoon kosher salt

4 (6- to 8-ounce) orange roughy fillets

TACOS
12 to 15 corn tortillas
1 white onion, diced
½ bunch cilantro, minced
1 Haas avocado, cut into chunks
Grated cheese (whatever you like!)
Romaine lettuce, shredded
Seafood Salsa (recipe page 37)

Whisk together all marinade ingredients. Rinse the fish under very cold water and dry with paper towel. Marinate the fish for 30 minutes, turning often. Grill the fish until done at center, drizzling with marinade as the fish is turned. Remove fish from grill and cut into bite-size pieces. Warm the tortillas on a comal or skillet, place a few pieces of fish in each tortilla, and let your guests add whatever they like.

Serves 6 to 8.

blackened swordfish steaks

Blackened fish is not an age-old Cajun recipe. It was developed by the world-famous chef and one of the people responsible for the Cajun food craze that hit the entire world in the '80s, Paul Prudhomme. Serve with Cajun Rice (recipe page 43).

2 swordfish steaks not more than
¾-inch thick
1 stick unsalted butter, melted

SPICE MIX
1 tablespoon paprika
2½ teaspoons kosher salt
1 teaspoon onion powder
1 teaspoon garlic powder
1 teaspoon ground cayenne
1 teaspoon freshly ground black pepper
1 teaspoon white pepper
½ teaspoon oregano
½ teaspoon thyme

GARNISH
fresh oregano
fresh thyme
lemon wedges
unsalted butter, melted

Due to the intense heat and smoke involved in this dish, we do not suggest you cook it indoors. Remember that in a commercial kitchen, directly above the stove, is an automatic fire-extinguishing system. Likewise, keep children away while performing this task and be careful.

Heat a large cast-iron skillet or griddle over high heat, until very hot, at least 5 minutes. Rinse the swordfish quickly under cold water and dry with a paper towel. Dip in melted better, coating both sides. Mix spices together and sprinkle over both sides of the fish, gently patting with your hands.

Place both swordfish steaks in the skillet and top with 1 teaspoon melted butter. Be careful, as steaks may flare up. Cook until the bottom side is crisp and just lightly charred, 1 to 3 minutes, depending on the thickness of the fish. Gently turn fish and top with 1 teaspoon melted butter. Cook the same as the other side, about 2 minutes, or until done. Transfer to warm dinner plates and sprinkle top of fish with a little finely chopped fresh thyme and oregano and place lemon wedge and ramekin of melted butter on the side. Serve immediately.

Serves 2.

opposite: *Blackened Swordfish Steaks (recipe above).*

seviche

Seviche is a great light treat on those hot summer days when you just don't feel like cooking. If you've avoided seviche thinking that it's raw fish, think again. The acid in the lime juice cooks the fish. Seviche is so refreshing!

1 pound fresh red snapper fillets,
rinsed well and paper towel–dried,
cut into ½-inch cubes
1 cup freshly squeezed Key lime juice
3 plum tomatoes, peeled and seeded
1 Haas avocado, cut into ½-inch cubes
2 diced serrano peppers
3 tablespoons safflower oil
3 scallions, finely chopped
1 clove minced garlic
½ teaspoon freshly grated ginger root
½ cup chopped cilantro, loosely packed
Kosher salt to taste
1 teaspoon balsamic vinegar

In a glass or ceramic container mix the lime and fish. Cover and refrigerate for 6 to 8 hours. Mix all other ingredients except avocado. Let flavors blend for ½ hour, gently fold in avocado, and serve.

Serves 6 to 8.

beef

Northern Mexico, more than anything, is ranching country. This is where many of our favorite Sonoran and Mexican dishes come from. The recipes found in this section are some of my most requested.

sonoran pot roast

Just like Mom made down on the farm (That is, if Mom lived on a little farm in northern Mexico!).

1 tablespoon safflower oil
1 (3- to 5-pound) pot roast
1 white onion, diced
4 cloves garlic, minced
3 shallots, minced
½ cup zinfandel wine
(don't even dream of using white zinfandel!)
4 beets, peeled and quartered
5 carrots, washed and cut into
2-inch sections
1 cabbage, cored and cut in half
1½ pounds small new potatoes
½ bunch Italian parsley,
rinsed and chopped
½ bunch cilantro, rinsed and chopped
Kosher salt to taste
Freshly ground black pepper to taste
2 teaspoons chile powder made from:
1 chipotle chile, seeded and ground
1 ancho chile, seeded and ground

Place pizza stone on grill, light burners, and turn to low. Allow grill to heat up slowly to about 350°. Turn off burners directly below pizza stone and adjust heat to maintain approximately 350°.

In a large, heavy Dutch oven, brown the roast, onion, garlic, and shallots in the safflower oil. Add all other ingredients and cover. Place on pizza stone and close grill lid. Bake for about 1 hour or until roast reaches an internal temperature of 132°. Serve with Mushroom-Chipotle Gravy (recipe page 50).

texas red chili!

I absolutely hate saying "Texas" when describing red chili, but I don't want you to mix this up with red chile from northern Mexico.

1½ pounds tri-tip, cubed
½ pound ground pork
2 large white onions (chopped)
2 (14-ounce) cans chicken broth
1 (8-ounce) can tomato sauce
¼ cup New Mexico mild red chile powder
1 teaspoon whole Mexican oregano
½ teaspoon ground cayenne pepper
3 cloves garlic finely minced
2 teaspoons cumin
Salt to taste
½ pound grated colby or Cheddar cheese
1 to 2 bottles Budweiser beer, as needed

In a large frying pan, brown the meat and half the onion; drain well and set aside.

Bring the chicken broth and tomato sauce to a boil in a large pot. Add the chile powder, oregano, cayenne pepper, garlic, cumin, and salt to the chicken broth. Boil over medium-high heat for 15 minutes. Add meat, reduce heat to medium, and boil for 30 minutes. Keep a good eye on your pot—do not let it get too thick. If it's getting thick, open one beer and pour half into the pot and the other half into the cook and reduce heat a little. Stir often. Don't let it stick or burn. Reduce heat to medium-low and simmer for 45 minutes or more. The chili should be lightly thick, like a cream soup, until the last 15 minutes of cooking. If the chili is too thick, repeat beer step as above. If it looks about right, pour the entire beer into the cook.

Serves 6.

smoked brisket caldillo (Mexican Brisket Stew)

You have got to try this wonderful stew. Besides, it's an excuse to spend a lazy day sipping cold beer and slow-smoking a brisket!

STEW

4 scallions, chopped

3 large plum tomatoes, cut into quarters

3 cloves garlic

1 white onion, cut into ½-inch cubes

½ red bell pepper, seeded and cut into slices

8 cups beef broth

2½ pounds new potatoes, cut into ½-inch cubes and rinsed

2 pounds Sonoran Mesquite-Smoked Brisket (recipe page 98), cut into ¾-inch cubes

4 poblano chiles, grill-roasted, peeled, seeded, and chopped

4 Anaheim chiles, grill-roasted, peeled, seeded, and chopped

2 tablespoons tomato paste

2 teaspoons ground cumin

1 teaspoon Mexican oregano

GARNISH

1-inch slices of Grilled-Roasted Corn on the Cob with Lime and Chile (recipe page 49)

Wedges of lime

Place pizza stone on grill, light burners, and turn to low. Allow grill to heat up slowly to about 350°. Turn off burners directly below pizza stone and adjust heat to maintain approximately 350°.

Place scallions, tomatoes, garlic, onion, and red bell on parchment paper on a cookie sheet and roast until browned and tender. Remove from grill and chop roasted garlic.

Place the broth in a large stock pot and simmer the potatoes, over medium heat, until tender. Reduce heat, add roasted vegetables and remaining ingredients (except corn and lime). Let simmer for 20 minutes for flavors to blend. Spoon into large soup bowls and garnish with Grilled Corn on the Cob with Lime and Chile.

Makes enough for 8 hungry hombres.

texas-style mesquite-barbecued brisket

In my mind, slow-smoked brisket is as good as it gets. Proper smoking calls for hours of sitting out by the smoker, sipping cold beer, and tempting your guests (who are being bathed in a wondrous aroma) by telling them that the brisket is almost done!

Brisket
1 cup of Texas Barbecue Rub (recipe page 66) for every 5 pounds of brisket
2 cups of Western Barbecue Sauce (recipe page 67) for every 5 pounds of brisket
(Don't even dream of putting the sauce on the meat before it's cooked)
Fresh baked French bread or onion buns

Rub the Brisket thoroughly with the rub and let stand at room temperature for 1 hour.

This is where a big covered grill or a two-chamber smoker comes in handy. Build your fire on one side of the grill (or in the lower chamber) and cook your meat on the other. If your grill or smoker has a thermometer, keep the temperature between 190° and 220°. In other words, a little pile of coals that you constantly feed a little Mesquite charcoal to. Place the brisket on the grill, fat side up, and close the lid. The process for this famous dish is to slow-cook your brisket for a minimum of 8 and as many as 10 hours, turning every 2 to 3 hours. When the brisket is done, slice thin and serve on bread with barbecue sauce on the side.

opposite: *Brisket with Tri-tip Marinade (recipe page 62). The trick to being a pro at smoking meats is patience. Heat your smoker to about 215°, toss the brisket in and relax. My producer, Bruce Jones, says this is the best tasting piece of meat he has ever eaten.*

sonoran mesquite-smoked brisket

This dish gives the savory flavors of smoked brisket our famous Sonoran twist!

Brisket (make enough for dinner and some
extra for Smoked Brisket Caldillo)
1 cup of Sonoran Brisket Rub (recipe page
63) for every 5 pounds of brisket
2 cups of Sonoran Brisket Marinade (recipe
page 63) for every 5 pounds of brisket

Rub the brisket thoroughly with the Sonoran Brisket Rub and let stand at room temperature for 1 hour.

Light a small pile of pure mesquite charcoal (not briquettes) in the lower chamber of a two-chamber smoker. Maintain a hood temperature of about 190°. The idea is a little pile of coals that you constantly feed a little mesquite charcoal to. Place the brisket on the upper rack, fat side up, and close the lid. Slow-cook your brisket for a minimum of 8 and as many as 10 hours, turning and basting every 2 to 3 hours. When the brisket is done, thinly slice and serve on bread with barbecue sauce on the side.

steak oau poivre-serrano

A juicy fillet of beef with a cognac cream sauce and chiles too!

3 tablespoons black peppercorns
4 (6-ounce) beef fillets, 1½ inches thick
1 tablespoon safflower oil
2 tablespoons butter
⅓ cup cognac
1 cup beef stock
½ cup heavy cream
Salt to taste (about 1 teaspoon)
2 serrano chiles, sliced paper thin

Wrap peppercorns in a clean dish towel. Crush with a heavy skillet or mallet. (Peppercorns should be crushed, not ground.) Roll fillets in ½ of the crushed pepper to coat. Grill to medium rare.

While steaks are grilling, sauté remaining ½ of the pepper in oil and butter. Add cognac to hot pan, *carefully* ignite with a long match, and allow all alcohol to burn off, approximately 1 minute (fire can be extinguished with pan lid). Add beef stock and simmer until reduced by half, about 4 minutes. Add cream and continue to simmer until thick, stirring occasionally. Salt to taste and drizzle over steaks. Top each steak with 4 to 6 slices of serrano and serve.

Serves 4.

grill-baked enchiladas

Here in the Sonoran Desert, we eat a lot of enchiladas. They are easy and a great dish to make outside on the grill. As with many dishes, you just need to know a few tricks!

1 warm corn tortilla per enchilada
Canola oil for coating pan
1 cup enchilada sauce per 4 enchiladas
1½ tablespoons of whatever filling you
like per enchilada: cooked beef,
cooked chicken, or cheese

Place pizza stone on grill, light burners, and turn to low. Allow grill to heat up slowly to about 350°, turn off burners directly below pizza stone, and adjust heat to maintain approximately 350°.

Warm up your corn tortillas on a lightly oiled comal or frying pan. Coat the bottom of a baking dish with enchilada sauce. On a warm corn tortilla place 1½ tablespoons filling. Roll up the enchilada and place in the baking dish seam side down. Repeat until baking dish is full. Top with remaining enchilada sauce and place on pizza stone for 20 to 25 minutes depending on your filling. In last 5 minutes of grill-baking, top with cheese.

Serve 2 to 3 enchiladas per guest.

tamales

Tamales are fun and easy. If you've never had a fresh homemade one you are in for a real treat!

1 package dried corn husks
1 (2-pound) pork roast
Kosher salt and freshly ground black pepper
3 cloves garlic, sliced very thin
Safflower oil
1 (14-ounce) can beef broth
⅓ cup red New Mexico chile powder
(hot or mild, your choice)
2 teaspoons Mexican oregano
Masa harina*
Shortening
Roasted green chiles, cut into strips
Hominy
Spanish olives

Soak corn husks in warm water overnight.

Season pork roast with salt and pepper and roast on grill until roast reaches internal temperature of 165°. Let cool and cut into ½-inch cubes.

Make red sauce. Sauté garlic in safflower oil until translucent. Add beef broth, New Mexico chile powder, and 2 teaspoons Mexican oregano. Bring to a boil over medium heat, reduce heat, and simmer until sauce reduces by ⅓. Add pork and simmer until sauce is thick and coats pork, stirring constantly.

Make Masa in blender following manufacturer's instructions on package. I use about ⅓ less shortening than called for.

Assemble and steam. Spoon 1 to 2 tablespoons of prepared masa onto each husk, add 1 tablespoon meat, then whatever you like. I add a strip of roasted green chile, a little hominy, and a Spanish olive. Roll the tamale up, tie the ends with a strip of corn husk, and steam, standing up, for 2 ½ hours.

Ask your grocer.

shredded beef for tacos or burritos

Tacos made with hamburger are nothing compared to good shredded beef!

1 to 2 pounds chuck roast
1 tablespoon red wine vinegar
Salt and freshly ground black pepper
Canola oil for coating pan
2 roasted poblano chiles, peeled and diced
2 cloves garlic, minced
½ white onion, diced

Place pizza stone on grill, light burners, and turn to low. Allow grill to heat up slowly to about 300°. Turn off burners directly below pizza stone and adjust heat to maintain approximately 300°.

Place the roast in a heavy roasting dish. Sprinkle the vinegar over the roast. Season with salt and pepper. Place on the pizza stone and slow-cook for 1½ to 2 hours.

Remove roast from heat and allow to cool down a little. Depending on how tender the roast is, either shred with a fork or cut into strips and then shred by hand. Place the beef in a lightly oiled nonstick pan and add chiles, garlic, and onion. Sauté until onions and garlic are soft. Use in tacos or burritos.

Makes enough meat for 12 to 15 tacos or 4 really big burritos.

poultry

In this chapter we really see just how versatile the grill can be. How about crispy, juicy, fried chicken on the grill, or a hearty Grill-Roasted Chicken Cacciatore? On that special night you can also try your hand at Grill-Roasted Duck Grand Marnier. Your friends and family will be amazed.

lynn's lemon chicken

My neighbor Lynn is the best cook I know. She says her family has this simple dish about once a week.

2 whole chickens, cut up and salted lightly
2 cups fresh squeezed lemon juice
1 cup extra virgin olive oil
1 tablespoon Red wine vinegar
3 cloves garlic, minced
1 teaspoon greek oregano
Kosher salt to taste
Fresh ground black pepper to taste
½ bunch Italian parsley, minced

Start grilling chicken, meanwhile whisk together lemon juice, olive oil, vinegar, garlic, oregano. salt and pepper. Once chicken starts to brown, dip each piece in the lemon sauce and return to the grill. Fully cook chicken while basting with lemon sauce.

Remove chicken from grill and bring lemon sauce back to a low boil for three minutes and add parsley.

Serve pieces of chicken covered with sauce. This dish goes well with lemon risotto and fresh steamed broccoli.

Makes 8 servings.

chicken and smoked-ham jambalaya

Jambalaya is a wonderful spicy Cajun dish. I always make a batch when I want to use up any leftover smoked meats or poultry.

2½ tablespoons sweet butter
¾ pound smoked ham, cut into bite-size pieces (about 3 cups)
¾ pound cooked chicken meat, cut into bite-size pieces (about 2 cups)
½ cup minced poblano chile
½ cup minced celery
¼ cup minced white onion
¼ cup minced shallots
2 cloves garlic, minced
½ cup tomato sauce
½ cup red bell pepper, minced
½ cup minced celery
½ cup minced white onion
1 cup peeled and chopped tomatoes
2½ cups chicken broth
1½ cups converted rice

JAMBALAYA SPICE MIX
1½ teaspoons cayenne pepper
1½ teaspoons white pepper
1½ teaspoons kosher salt
¾ teaspoon ground thyme
½ teaspoon freshly ground black pepper
¼ teaspoon ground sage
¼ teaspoon Greek oregano
2 whole bay leaves

Place pizza stone on grill, light burners, and turn to low. Allow grill to slowly heat up to about 350°, turn off burners directly below pizza stone, and adjust heat to maintain approximately 350°.

Sauté the ham and chicken in the butter for about 5 minutes. Add spice mix, poblano, celery, onion, shallots, and garlic. Sauté until onions are soft. Combine ham/chicken mixture with all other ingredients in a casserole dish and grill-bake, uncovered, for 1 hour. Serve with Creole Sauce (recipe page 57).

Serves 6.

filé gumbo with grill-roasted chicken and andouille sausage

If you like grill-roasted meats and spicy foods, you are going to absolutely love this famous Cajun dish!

RUB
½ cup Hungarian paprika
2 tablespoons kosher salt
1 tablespoon brown sugar
2 teaspoons cayenne pepper
1 teaspoon thyme
1 teaspoon granulated garlic

4 chicken legs
2 chicken thighs
2 chicken wings

GUMBO
¼ cup sweet butter
2 tablespoons filé powder
1½ cups minced white onion
1½ cups minced red bell pepper
1½ cups minced celery
1 tablespoon Trappey's Red Hot Sauce
½ teaspoon white pepper
½ teaspoon Greek oregano
½ teaspoon cayenne pepper
½ teaspoon kosher salt
½ teaspoon granulated garlic
1 cup tomato sauce
1 cup tomatoes, peeled and seeded
6 cups chicken broth
1 pound okra, sliced into ½-inch rings
½ pound andouille sausage, sliced

Mix the rub ingredients together, rub on outside of chicken, and slowly grill-roast, with a medium fire, until fully cooked. Set aside.

Melt the butter in a large stock pot over medium-high heat. Add filé powder, onion, bell pepper, celery, hot sauce, white pepper, oregano, cayenne, salt, and granulated garlic. Sauté until soft. Add tomato sauce, tomatoes, chicken broth, and okra. Bring to a boil, reduce heat, add sausage and chicken; simmer for at least 1 hour. Serve with Cajun Rice (recipe page 43).

Serves 6.

sonoran chicken salad

A great light salad with all the flavors of the Sonoran Desert!

DRESSING
¾ cup olive oil
1½ tablespoons lemon juice
1½ tablespoons lime juice
1 teaspoon Dijon mustard
2 cloves garlic, finely minced
½ teaspoon Greek oregano
½ teaspoon Italian seasoning
Pinch crushed red chile
1 chile de arbol
¼ teaspoon salt

SALAD
1 pound cooked, deboned, and skinned
chicken, shredded
1 avocado, diced
1 cup jicama, julienned
1 red bell pepper, diced
½ bunch fresh cilantro, washed
and chopped
¼ cup green onions, chopped
½ cup white corn
1 head Romaine lettuce

Whisk dressing ingredients together and let stand for at least 1 hour, allowing flavors to blend. Combine all other ingredients except lettuce, gently mix in dressing, and let chill. Serve on a bed of Romaine lettuce.

Serves 6 nicely.

grill-fried chicken

I made this dish to prove that it could be done. It's now a family favorite.

3 cups Kellogg's Corn Flake Crumbs
2 teaspoons kosher salt
1 teaspoon granulated garlic
1 teaspoon paprika
1 free-range frying chicken, cut up*
1 (12-ounce) can evaporated milk
½ stick butter, melted

Preheat the grill to 375°. Turn off center burners and adjust the outside burners to maintain heat. In a mixing bowl, mix together the corn flake crumbs, salt, garlic, and paprika. Dip the chicken, one piece at a time, first in the evaporated milk and then in the crumb mixture. Place in a baking dish skin side up. Drizzle very lightly with butter. Place the baking dish in the center of grill, with no heat directly below the baking dish. Bake for about 1 hour, until chicken is dark golden brown and temperature at center of breast is 160°.

Serves 6.

Do not try this recipe with cheaper grades of chicken: It will be a greasy mess.

opposite: *Grilled-fried Chicken (recipe above) with buttermilk biscuits.*

mesquite-grilled jamaican jerk chicken

Consider this dish culinary bungee jumping. It's like giving your taste buds a ride in a rocket sled straight to Hell. (It's also one of my favorites.)

JERK PASTE
8 to 10 habanero chiles with seeds, puréed
2 tablespoons powdered allspice
3 scallions, chopped
1 teaspoon ground cinnamon
1 teaspoon ground nutmeg
1 teaspoon salt
¼ cup yellow mustard
3 tablespoons freshly squeezed Key lime juice
2 tablespoons freshly squeezed orange juice
2 teaspoons mustard seeds
2 tablespoons white vinegar

6 chicken leg-thigh quarters
Pure mesquite charcoal (not briquettes)

Blend the jerk paste ingredients to a consistency a little thinner than catsup (if too thick, thin with a little more lime juice or water). Coat chicken, cover, and let stand for at least 4 hours to marry the flavors.

Slow-smoke chicken in a two-chamber smoker. Cook slow for a couple of hours: This dish is best well done. When chicken is done (165°), cut pieces in half at the joint and serve immediately.

Serves 8 to 10 brave souls.

grill-roasted duck grand marnier

When you really want to show off your grilling talents, this is the perfect dish. It's not only beautiful, but the combination of the spicy Asian citrus flavor and the roast duck is a real gourmet treat!

1 (4- to 5-pound) duck
Kosher salt
Freshly ground black pepper
3 sprigs fresh thyme
1 celery rib, with leaves, roughly chopped
½ small white onion, quartered
1 shallot, chopped
1 medium orange, quartered
Paprika
¼ cup Grand Marnier

Place pizza stone on grill, light burners, and turn to low. Allow grill to slowly heat up to about 350°, turn off burners directly below pizza stone, and adjust heat to maintain approximately 350°.

Rinse the duck well. Remove neck, giblets, and tail. Rub the inside cavity of the duck with salt and pepper. Fill the duck's inside cavity with a combination of thyme sprigs, celery, onion, shallot, and orange quarters. Lightly salt, pepper, and then paprika the exterior of the duck.

Place a large baking dish on the pizza stone, and then a wire rack on top of the baking dish. Place the duck on the rack* breast side down. Grill-roast for 45 minutes, and then turn with tongs, breast side up. Drizzle with Grand Marnier. Roast for 45 minutes to 1 hour, or until the leg joints wiggle easily when pulled and the internal temperature at the center of the thickest part of the thigh is 165°. Remove from heat. Cut duck in half lengthwise and allow to cool down enough to touch. Remove breast and back bones and serve topped with Spicy Asian Kumquat Sauce (recipe page 69).

Serves 4.

*Due to the extremely high fat content of ducks, it is necessary to use a drip pan. Keep an eye on this the first few times you try it, and be careful. It is not uncommon to find that the cause of a kitchen fire was a duck in the oven!

grill-roasted chicken cacciatore

Originally this dish was called "Cacciatoria," which meant "Hunter's wife's chicken" in reference to the traditional, hearty dish served by the hunter's wife the night before the hunt.

1 whole fresh chicken, cut up

SAUCE
¼ cup extra-virgin olive oil
2 medium white onions, peeled and chopped
6 cloves garlic, peeled and minced
1 cup cabernet sauvignon
3 cups peeled, seeded, and diced plum tomatoes
3 cups beef broth
1 (8-ounce) can tomato sauce
Juice of ½ lemon
3 tablespoons sweet butter
¼ cup fresh Italian parsley, finely minced
1 bay leaf
1 teaspoon minced rosemary
Salt and pepper to taste
¼ pound Italian brown mushrooms, rinsed and sliced
¼ cup medium green olives, pitted

GARNISH
1 tablespoon fresh Italian parsley
Grated fresh Romano cheese

Grill chicken over medium-high heat until chicken is well browned, but do not fully cook.

In a large sauté pan over medium-high heat, heat oil. Cook onions until soft, add garlic, and cook a minute or two more to release flavor into the oil. Add chicken and stir. Add wine and simmer until liquid reduces to almost nothing (be careful not to burn). Add tomatoes, 2 cups beef broth, tomato sauce, lemon juice, butter, herbs, and salt and pepper. Simmer for at least 45 minutes, then add mushrooms and olives. Simmer for 10 minutes more. As sauce reduces, replace liquid with beef broth a little at a time. Garnish with parsley and Romano cheese. Serve with orzo.

Serves 8.

opposite: *Grill-Roasted Chicken Cacciatore (recipe above) with Grill-Roasted, Stuffed Portobello Mushrooms (recipe page 117).*

meatless (eggs, vegetables, and pasta)

In this section you'll find some fantastic recipes for those times you just don't feel like eating meat. They are light, delicious and most of all, easy: The perfect cure for those dog days of summer.

huevos rancheros

This is the only way to start a Saturday morning, unless you make a good menudo.

Nonstick cooking spray
2 5-inch corn tortillas per guest
2 extra-large eggs per guest
Refried beans, hot
Smoky Ranchero Salsa, warm
(recipe page 38)
Queso Fresco or feta cheese, crumbled
Chopped lettuce and avocado slices for
garnish

In a nonstick skillet over medium heat, using nonstick cooking spray, lightly fry the tortillas until soft and pliable. Put the tortillas in a tortilla warmer or on a plate and cover with a clean dish towel. Fry the eggs.

Place two tortillas on a dinner plate on top of a scoop of refried beans. Place one fried egg on each tortilla. Spoon on 2 tablespoons warm Smoky Ranchero Salsa per tortilla and top with crumbled cheese. Garnish with chopped lettuce and avocado slices.

grill-roasted, stuffed portobello mushrooms

These delicious stuffed mushrooms can be used as a great side dish or a juicy, light main course. Your friends won't believe that you made them on the grill.

10 large portobello mushrooms
3 tablespoons unsalted butter
1 bunch green onions, cleaned and minced
1 (10-ounce) package frozen, chopped spinach, thawed and drained
2 tablespoons sundried tomatoes, minced
½ tablespoon Greek oregano
½ teaspoon nutmeg
½ cup seasoned bread crumbs
1½ cups freshly grated Romano cheese
4 large eggs
¾ cup heavy cream
1 teaspoon kosher salt
½ teaspoon freshly ground black pepper
Pinch of cayenne pepper
Vegetable oil spray

Place pizza stone on grill, light burners, and turn to low. Allow grill to slowly heat up to about 400°, turn off burners directly below pizza stone, and adjust heat to maintain approximately 400°.

Remove the stems from the mushrooms and discard. Chop 2 of the mushrooms. In a medium skillet over medium heat, sauté the chopped mushrooms in the butter, adding the onions, spinach, sundried tomatoes, oregano, and nutmeg, until mushrooms are golden brown. Stir in bread crumbs and sauté for 3 more minutes. Mixture should be very dry. Remove from heat and allow to cool. Add about ⅔ of the cheese and stir in the eggs, cream, salt, pepper, and cayenne. Lightly spray tops (rounded part) of the mushrooms with vegetable oil spray and place the mushrooms top down on a cookie sheet or baking dish. Spoon in filling to evenly coat but do not fill as full as possible and sprinkle remaining cheese over top. Place baking dish on pizza stone and roast until mushrooms are tender, about 20 minutes. Remove from grill and serve.

Serves 8.

fettuccine and fresh pesto

In the late spring and early summer when the basil is full of flavor and ready to harvest, we always have a pesto party. It goes something like this: A few good friends, a good red wine, and homemade pesto. It's a night that you and your friends won't soon forget!

1 pound basil leaves (more or less)
3 tablespoons pine nuts
1 tablespoon walnuts
3 cloves garlic
½ cup freshly grated Parmesan cheese,
plus some for serving
¼ cup freshly grated Romano cheese
2 ounces chopped fresh spinach, rinsed
and drained
½ cup extra-virgin olive oil
Salt and freshly ground pepper to taste
1 (16-ounce) box fettuccine
noodles, cooked

Mix all ingredients except noodles, salt, and pepper together in a large bowl. Place ⅔ of the mixture in a food processor and blend until smooth. Add last ⅓ of mixture to food processor and blend until lightly coarse. The combination of well-blended with coarsely blended pesto gives the sauce the correct feel and releases all the flavor of the basil. Salt and pepper to taste. Lightly butter a small saucepan and over a low heat, gently warm the pesto.

Serve approximately one tablespoon of warm pesto in the center of a serving of hot, buttered fettuccine noodles. Allow your guests to toss their own pesto. Serve with freshly ground black pepper and freshly ground Parmesan cheese.

Serves 4 to 6.

pomodoro cruda made with orange vine-ripe tomatoes on angel-hair pasta

In the spring your grocer offers "Vine Ripe" tomatoes: red, yellow, and orange. They cost a little more, but "Boy, howdy" are they worth it. This dish, served with a little red wine, is one of my all-time favorite light, summer meals.

POMODORO SAUCE

3 cups vine-ripe, orange tomatoes (red will also work well, but remove the seeds), cored and cut into ½-inch chunks
½ cup extra-virgin olive oil, plus extra for cooking pasta
2 cloves garlic, pressed
1 teaspoon crushed red pepper
20 fresh basil leaves, with buds, torn, not chopped
Freshly ground Romano cheese to taste
Salt and freshly ground pepper to taste

1 (12-ounce) box angel-hair pasta

Toss all ingredients together except the pasta. Cover, refrigerate, and let stand for 30 minutes for flavors to blend.

Cook the pasta, drain, add a little olive oil, and toss. While pasta is still warm, divide between 4 to 6 plates (depending on appetite) and top with the cold Pomodoro Sauce. Offer more Romano at table.

Serves 4 to 6.

Saying it's a hot day in Arizona is

like saying it's a rainy day in Seattle.

It's always hot in Arizona, so we take our drinks seriously.

drinks

Here are a few of my favorites that are guaranteed to

satisfy even a Sonoran-Desert thirst.

bloody mary jane

I made this version of the great American classic in honor of Mary Jane Wylan, the lovely wife of Dave DeWitt, co-writer of *The Whole Chile Pepper Book*.

2 ounces vodka (use good vodka, you'll taste the difference)
4 ounces tomato juice
1 teaspoon prepared horseradish
Juice of ½ medium lemon
2 dashes Tabasco Habanero Sauce
1 dash Louisiana Hot Sauce
Sprinkle of celery salt
½ teaspoon black pepper
Salt to taste
Celery stalk for garnish

Combine drink ingredients in a shaker with ice and shake. Strain into glass of ice; garnish with a celery stalk.

Makes 1.

cervezarita negra

Life in this part of the world simply would not be the same without tequila and dark Mexican beer. This refreshing cocktail offers the very best of both of these delightful beverages.

1 ounce Tequila Blanco
1 ounce Grand Marnier
Juice of 1 Key lime
12 ounces Negra Modelo Dark Ale

Pour beer into a frosted mug. Mix liquor and lime juice together, gently pour over beer.

Makes 1.

classic margarita

Margaritas made with regular lime juice cannot compare with those made with Key limes. So before your next party, ask your grocer to order some of these little beauties.

1½ ounces your favorite tequila
1½ ounces Cointreau liqueur
Juice of 2 fresh Key limes

Shake with ice and serve.

Makes 1.

irish coffee

In this part of the Sonoran Desert, we only have about twenty really cold nights a year, but when we do I pour one of these and think of my departed Irish grandmother, Margaret Rose Brannen.

1 ounce Bushmill's Irish Whiskey
1 pot of fresh brewed coffee (not flavored)
Fresh cream to taste
1 teaspoon sugar
Fresh whipped cream

Pour whiskey into a large coffee mug. Add coffee, and a little cream if you like. Add sugar to take the edge off the whiskey. Top with whipped cream.

Makes 1.

la reserva cocktail

Elegant Sonoran!

Juice of 1 Key lime
Jose Quervo La Reserva Tequila
Dash of Mandarin Napoleon

Rim martini glass with lime and fill with ice. Gently fill glass with La Reserva, top with remaining lime juice and Mandarin Napoleon.

Makes 1.

prickly pear lemonade

When I have friends from out of town over on a hot day I make this easy lemonade. Not only is it delicious, it's also a great conversation starter.

2 cups fresh lemon juice, strained
1 tablespoon prickly pear syrup
4 cups water
½ cup sugar
1 lemon, thinly sliced, for garnish

In a large pitcher mix lemon juice, prickly pear syrup, water, and sugar; stir until sugar dissolves.

Add ice and lemon slices; serve.

Makes 1½ quarts.

stevie ray

I made this excellent drink in honor of the great American Blues legend Stevie Ray Vaughn. Be careful: This refreshing drink, like his music, is powerful and goes down smooth and easy.

2 ounces Don Julio Silver Tequila
½ ounce Blue Curacao
½ ounce Mandarin Napoleon
Juice of 1 Key lime

Shake Ingredients with ice; strain, and serve in a martini glass.

Makes 1.

tequila martini

Manhattan meets Mexico City, while wearing a tux.

1½ ounces Tequila Añejo
Dash of Mandarin Napoleon
Dash of Blue Curacao
1 pimento-stuffed olive

Shake liquids together and serve in a martini glass with ice and an olive.

Makes 1.

My whole philosophy on desserts

was handed down to me by my

father. When I was a little kid he told me: "Always eat

dessert before dinner. You never know, you might die

during dinner and then you would miss out." If by good

fortune you make it through dinner unharmed, you can

celebrate by having dessert again.

almond kahlúa flan

Yumm . . .

2 cups milk
¾ cup plus 2 tablespoons sugar
2 whole eggs plus 1 egg yolk, lightly beaten
½ tablespoon Kahlúa
1 teaspoon instant espresso powder
Pinch of kosher salt
½ teaspoon vanilla extract

GARNISH
Orange zest
Kahlúa
Slivered almonds

Place pizza stone on the grill, light burners, and turn to low. Allow grill to heat up slowly to about 350°, turn off burners directly below pizza stone, and adjust heat to maintain approximately 350°.

Scald the milk in a double boiler on the stove. Place ¾ cup of the sugar in skillet over medium-high heat on the stove. Be careful, as this a good place to get burned. Stir the sugar constantly while it melts and turns medium brown. Remove from heat, pour to coat bottom of four 4-ounce ramekins. Allow to cool.

Whisk together the eggs, 2 remaining tablespoons of sugar, ½ tablespoon Kahlúa, espresso powder, salt, and vanilla extract. Slowly whisk into the hot milk. Pour through a strainer into a bowl and spoon into the ramekins until almost full.

Place a large pot with a lid on the grill. Place the ramekins in the pot and add 1 inch of warm water, creating a water bath. (Be careful not to pour any water into the ramekins.) Cover and grill-bake for 20 to 25 minutes, or until a knife inserted in the center of the flan comes out clean. Drizzle with a little Kahlúa and top with orange zest and slivered almonds.

Serves 4.

jamaican rum-glazed grilled peaches

A tropical dessert for those warm spring nights.

GLAZE
1 cup dark Jamaican rum
¼ cup dark brown sugar
1 tablespoon sweet butter
2 teaspoons minced ginger
½ cup molasses
1½ teaspoons allspice
Pinch of cinnamon
Pinch of mace

4 ripe peaches, halved and pitted

Combine all ingredients except peaches in a small saucepan and simmer for 5 minutes, stirring often. Let cool.

Grill peaches, cut side down, over medium heat for 3 minutes per side (or until soft); brush with sauce and grill for 1 more minute per side.

Serves 6 to 8.

lychee-coconut granita

Lychees are a delicious little Asian fruit that taste a little like a very sweet grapefruit.

½ cup sugar
½ cup water
1 (20-ounce) can crushed pineapple, with juice
2 (11-ounce) cans lychees, puréed
½ cup fresh Key lime juice
½ cup freshly grated coconut
½ cup sake
Zest of 1 lime
1 pint fresh fruits or berries

In a small saucepan, bring sugar and water to a boil. Remove from heat. Add pineapple, lychees, lime juice, coconut, sake, and lime zest. Stir well and pour into a shallow baking pan. Place in freezer for 4 hours. When frozen, scrape with a fork to create crystals. Top with fresh fruit or berries.

Serves 8 to 10.

chocolate espresso pudding

Use the best quality semi-sweet chocolate in this recipe. You'll taste the difference.

½ cup sugar
3 tablespoons unsweetened cocoa powder
2½ tablespoons cornstarch
¼ teaspoon salt
1 large egg
2 egg yolks
2 cups milk
4 ounces semi-sweet chocolate, chopped
2 tablespoons unsalted butter
1 tablespoon instant espresso powder
1 teaspoon vanilla extract
Whipped cream for topping

Mix together the sugar, cocoa, cornstarch, and salt in a bowl. In a separate bowl, whisk together the eggs and egg yolks. Pour the eggs into the cocoa mixture and whisk until it forms a smooth paste.

Scald the milk in a medium saucepan over medium heat. Remove from heat. While whisking, add ½ cup of the hot milk to the cocoa mixture; continue whisking until smooth. While whisking, pour the cocoa mixture back into the hot milk. Whisk until smooth. Return to medium heat and continue whisking for 5 to 6 minutes, until pudding begins to boil. Remove from heat and whisk in the chocolate, butter, espresso, and vanilla extract; whisk until smooth. With a rubber spatula, spoon the pudding into a glass bowl and allow to cool to room temperature. Cover with plastic and refrigerate until fully chilled.

Serves 4.

prickly pear-margarita sorbet

I always seem to pour way more tequila than is called for in this dessert. . . . But my guests never complain!

2 tablespoons 100% Agave Tequila
2½ cups very cold bottled water
1 cup sugar
¼ cup corn syrup
Juice and pulp from 6 Key limes, seeds removed
Zest of 1 lime
1 tablespoon prickly-pear syrup
Mint leaves and lime wedges for garnish

Stir together the tequila, water, sugar, and corn syrup until sugar dissolves. Stir in the lime juice, lime zest, and prickly-pear syrup. Transfer ingredients to an ice-cream maker and follow manufacturer's instructions.

Put the sorbet in the freezer for 10 minutes before serving. It will be hard enough to scoop into servings. Garnish with mint leaves and lime wedges.

Makes 6.

raspberry sauce

This easy sauce is great on fruit, ice cream, or pound cake.

2 cups plus 2 tablespoons water
½ cup sugar
1 (12-ounce) bag frozen raspberries
Juice of ½ lemon
1 tablespoon cornstarch

In a small saucepan, bring 2 cups of the water and sugar to a boil. Add the raspberries and lemon juice and mash with a fork or potato masher. Mix the cornstarch with remaining 2 tablespoons water and whisk into the berries. Simmer for 5 minutes. Let cool and thicken before using.

Makes enough for 4 d'Anjou pears (recipe page 133).

grilled pineapple with pink grapefruit, lime, and dried-cherry glaze

When I really want to show off, I grill some pineapple and top it with this delicious glaze.

GLAZE
⅓ cup sugar
2 tablespoons water
¼ cup pink grapefruit juice
Juice of 4 limes
2 teaspoons dried mint

2 small to medium pineapples (they are sweeter than large pineapples), skin removed and cut into 1-inch, round slices
¼ cup fresh mint leaves, minced
¼ cup finely chopped dried cherries

In a small saucepan over medium heat, bring the sugar and water to a boil while whisking. As soon as sugar dissolves and syrup becomes clear, add grapefruit juice, lime juice, and dried mint. Reduce heat and simmer for 4 minutes, stirring occasionally. Remove from heat and let cool.

Grill pineapple slices over a medium fire until lightly charred, 3 to 4 minutes per side, depending on heat level. Just before removing from the grill, drizzle with a little glaze.

Place 2 slices of grilled pineapple on each plate. Stir the fresh mint into the glaze. Top each slice with a tablespoon of glaze. Sprinkle a teaspoon of dried cherries on each serving.

Serves 6 to 8.

blackberry cobbler

This is my Grandma Rose's famous recipe. Our family loves this mouth-watering dessert.

FILLING
4 (6-ounce) containers of fresh
blackberries
Juice of ½ lemon
1½ tablespoons cornstarch
¾ cup sugar

TOPPING
1 cup flour
¾ cup sugar
½ teaspoon salt
½ teaspoon baking powder
1 large egg
1 stick butter, melted

Preheat oven to 375°. In a small saucepan, bring 1 cup of water to a low boil. Place 6 ounces of the blackberries and lemon juice in a blender and purée. Add to the saucepan and simmer for 3 minutes. Remove from heat.

Put remaining berries in a bowl and carefully mix in cornstarch and sugar, trying not to break up berries. Carefully fold in the warm berry mixture. Spoon mixture into an 8 x 8-inch baking dish or a pie pan.

In a separate bowl, mix together flour, sugar, salt, and baking powder. Add egg and mix until crumbly. Sprinkle topping over blackberry mixture and drizzle with melted butter.

Bake for 45 minutes or until topping is a deep, golden brown. Serve with vanilla ice cream and good coffee.

Makes 8 to 10 servings.

grilled pears

Pears are great on the grill. Make sure to use a baking or poaching pear like d'Anjou.

4 d'Anjou pears
Vegetable oil spray

Cut pears in half lengthwise and remove seeds and stem. Spray with a light coat of vegetable oil and grill until brown and soft. Top with Raspberry Sauce (recipe page 131).

Serves 4.

opposite: *Grill-Baked Scalloped Potatoes (recipe page 53) and Blackberry Cobbler (recipe above) baking in adobe horno.*

grilled sweet potato, pecan tarts

We grow a lot of pecans here in Arizona. Your guests will love getting their own tart.

CRUST
¼ cup plus 2 tablespoons unsalted
butter, softened
¼ cup sugar
½ teaspoon salt
1 egg, well beaten
¼ cup cold milk
2 cups flour

FILLING
1 cup mashed baked sweet potato
pulp, cooled
¼ cup light brown sugar
2 tablespoons sugar
1 tablespoon vanilla extract
1 tablespoon unsalted butter
1 tablespoon heavy cream
½ of a well beaten egg
¼ teaspoon salt
¼ teaspoon cinnamon
⅛ teaspoon nutmeg
⅛ teaspoon allspice

SYRUP
¾ cup dark corn syrup
¾ cup sugar
1½ tablespoons unsalted butter, melted
2 teaspoons vanilla extract
2 medium eggs
Pinch of cinnamon
Pinch of salt

TOPPING
1 cup pecan halves

To make the crust, beat the butter, sugar, and salt with an electric mixer on high until smooth and creamy. Add the egg and beat on medium for 30 seconds. Add the milk and beat on high for 1½ minutes. Pour in the flour and mix on medium using a bread hook (if available) for 5 to 10 seconds and then on high for 5 seconds more. (Over-mixing will produce a tough tart crust.) Remove the dough and, on a lightly floured surface, pat it out into an 8-inch circle. Lightly flour both sides and wrap with plastic. Let rest for at least 1 hour in the refrigerator. Dough may be made the night before and will keep in the refrigerator for up to five days.

Combine all filling ingredients and mix with an electric mixer until smooth. Set aside.

In a medium mixing bowl, combine all syrup ingredients. Whisk until syrup is opaque and fully blended.

Place a 14-inch pizza stone in the gas grill and turn on high for 10 minutes. Turn off all burners except directly below the pizza stone. Reduce heat to low: You're looking for an internal temperature of 375° to 400°.

On a lightly floured surface roll out the dough to a thickness of between ⅛ and ¼ of an inch. Dough needs to be roughly 8½ inches wide by 13 to 14 inches long. Cut the dough into six 4½-inch squares. Gently place the dough in lightly oiled 4-inch tart pans (if the dough is too short, just roll it out a little more). Gently arrange the dough into the corners of the tart pans and fold excess dough to the outside. Using caution, roll the rolling pin across the top of the tart pans to trim dough.

(Continued on page 135)

Spoon sweet-potato filling into bottom ⅓ of tart pan. Place pecans in pan to cover sweet potato filling. Spoon in enough syrup to cover pecans but don't add so much that it spills out over the top. Pecans will rise to the top during baking.

Place the tarts on the pizza stone and bake for about 30 minutes. The top of the tart will become frothy and then caramelize. Remove tarts and let cool for 20 minutes. Serve with ice cream. I like them best the next morning with coffee.

Makes six 4-inch tarts.

white nectarine ice cream

This dessert is so delicious, words cannot explain. It's also great made with fresh peaches.

3 or 4 white nectarines, finely chopped
1¼ cups sugar
Juice of ½ lemon
2 large fresh eggs
2 cups heavy cream
1 cup fresh milk
1 teaspoon vanilla extract

In a mixing bowl, stir together nectarines, ½ cup of the sugar, and the lemon juice. Cover with plastic wrap and refrigerate for 2 hours, stirring every ½ hour.

Drain juice from nectarines, reserving juice, and re-refrigerate nectarines. In a mixing bowl, whisk eggs for about 2 minutes, until light and fluffy. Add the remaining sugar a little at a time while whisking. Continue to whisk for about 1 minute more, or until completely blended. Whisk in cream, milk, and vanilla. Stir in nectarine juice until fully blended. Transfer mixture to your ice-cream maker and follow manufacturer's instructions. A minute or two before ice cream is done, add nectarines. Enjoy.

Serves 4 to 6.

acknowledgments

Special thanks to the people that made this book possible.

To the guys that thought the show up, and make it all happen each week:

Bruce Jones, Don McClure, and Paul Hallowell.

To Barbara Holland and Muriel Hart.

To Lynn Damon, the best cook I know.

To Paul Elswick for knowing I was a writer before I did.

To Mike Rosenthal and everyone at the Hemophilia Association of Arizona.

To Andy Householder for helping me really understand flavors.

To Randy Smith for being there for me every minute in the past thirty-five years.

To Scott Maish for helping me think up Mad Coyote in the first place.

To Jim Ross for the seed money.

To Ryan Hall and the whole crew at "Crafting with Ma and Claire."

To Ed Fedoruk, Steve Pursell, Jerry Cohen, Mike Assad, and Bill Payne.

To the Vikings: Jason, Patrick, Gavin, Joe, Sparky, and Chantel.

Especially to David Grossman, for unselfishly teaching me how to work a room.

And last, but certainly not least, my friend, mentor, and the one who
got me a seat in the big game, Bob Boze Bell.

index

Mad Coyote Joe's love for Southwestern foods began as a child growing up in Arizona and developed while working in several Scottsdale and Phoenix restaurants. However, he really started his education on Sonoran grilling in 1987 as the owner of the Mad Coyote Spice Company, for which he developed fifty-four different spice products. Joe continued learning about Mexican cuisine while working with Hands Across the Border, a cultural exchange program, where he stayed in the private homes of farmers in northern Mexico. This experience was a natural transition into his current job as the host of the Southwestern TV show *The Sonoran Grill.*

In the mid-1990s, Joe served as host for the Mad Coyote Joe Annual Charity Cook-Off and Auction. Sponsored by The Chili Appreciation Society of America, it was the largest non-profit chili cook-off in Arizona history. For the past five years Joe has also served as head judge and master of ceremonies for the Xerox Southwest Salsa Challenge, which benefits the Hemophilia Association of Arizona. He is an honorary lifetime member of the International Chili Society, and has won numerous awards for his spice mixes and chili. Joe also contributes to *Chile Pepper Magazine* and *Fiery Foods Magazine.*

In addition to his love of Southwestern cuisine, Joe is also an avid guitar player who supports acoustic music in Arizona by performing, volunteering as a guitar teacher, and hosting open mike shows in his home town of Cave Creek, Arizona, where he lives with his wife, Kathy, and two children, Katie and Joey.